Adventures With Ploox
Book I: Risks, Wrecks and Roughnecks

the Brothers Armfinnigan

First published by Dog Ear Publishing
4010 W. 86th Street, Ste H
Indianapolis, IN 46268
www.dogearpublishing.net

ISBN: 978-145750-365-8

This book is printed on acid-free paper.

Printed in the United States of America

To the kids of Claresholm

Thanks for keeping the dream alive.

Part I

Freight Train Hoppin', Nickel Floppin'

CHAPTER 1

*N*icky Neill's tires hummed over the pavement, making that old familiar whirr. He'd loved that bike from the moment his dad gave it to him, the same dad who was now a missing person.

"Ploox, Ploox, looks so dumb, picks his nose, sucks his thumb!" Nicky Neill muttered the old playground chant as he hopped the curb near the intersection of Seventh and Main. "Pants are wet, snot is green, dumbest kid you've ever seen!" I must be crazy, he thought to himself, to want Ploox for something like this. "Ah, there it is," he gasped. "Ploox, you better be there." Up ahead the bus station loomed like an enemy bunker.

Nicky Neill hopped a final curb and sailed onto the dusty lot next to the Greyhound station. As he rode up to the main doorway he slammed on his brakes and leaned into the skid. Seconds later, he burst into the building.

"Ploox," he mumbled, breathless, "where the heck are you?"

The interior of the bus station was jumping. A rowdy group of college kids swarmed around a mountain of suitcases and steamer trunks. Blue cigarette smoke curled through the air and clung to the ceiling. On the opposite side of the room several families waited impatiently for their bus to arrive. Near the exit doors an old man sprawled across a bank of chairs, asleep with his mouth wide open. But there was no sign of Ploox.

Nicky Neill glanced at the ticket counter. A long line had formed behind the solitary open window. "Aaagh!" he gagged in horror. In the middle of the line, Mr. Plucowski stood erect and tall, hulking over everyone else. Ploox slouched beside him staring into space, his right thumb fixed firmly in his mouth and a blank expression tattooed across his face. He was crowding six feet himself and his wiry hair made him seem even taller, but next to his dad he was just another runt kid. Without warning, Mr. Plucowski delivered a swat to the back of his son's head and said, "I thought I told you to keep that thing outta your mouth. No thumb sucker I know of ever escaped sixth grade."

Nicky Neill wasn't quite ready to face off with Ploox's old man and what he'd just witnessed scared him even more. Still, he had no choice. He sucked down a lung full of stale air and made for the ticket line. As he approached, Mr. Plucowski stepped forward, closing the slack in the line. Sensing an opportunity, Nicky Neill slipped in beside his friend and hissed, "Ploox! Ploox!"

But Ploox didn't notice him. He was too busy rubbing the sore spot on the back of his head.

"Ploox!" Nicky Neill repeated, grabbing his friend's arm.

"Nicky Neill!" Ploox's deep, froggy voice hung in his throat. "Whutcha doin' here? This is the bus station!"

"I know. I came here looking for you."

"Huh?" Ploox took a long swipe at his leaky schnozz with the back of his wrist.

"Hey! Little Carpenter!" Mr. Plucowski's voice bellowed above the din and, for a split second, the entire station fell silent. "What the heck are you doin' here, boy?" He paused, but before Nicky Neill could answer he barked, "Whatever yer business, you ain't cuttin' in this here line."

"Oh, no, sir! I just dropped by to say so long to Ploox ... I mean, George!"

Mr. Plucowski eyeballed the boy suspiciously. Then one of his hands shot up to his face and delivered a toothpick to his mouth. Nicky Neill watched as he began to work the pick around his teeth. His fist was the size of a plucked turkey. Mr. P. had been a boxer in the Marine Corps and a war hero in Korea. The rumor was he still liked to fight, but at six feet, seven inches, no one had ever pushed the issue. "Uh, sir," Nicky Neill went on, "if it's okay with you I'll just talk with George a minute and then I'll be gone."

"Hmm, I reckon there ain't no harm in that, but don't be puttin' no silly notions in his head. I know all about yer schemin' an' such, buster. George is goin' away to school an' that's that!"

"Yessir! And I think it's a smart move."

"Yeah," he snorted, "I'm sure you do." Then he glanced at his wristwatch. "I gotta go to the can. George, you stay put. As for you, Carpenter," he shot Nicky Neill a look that stopped his heart, "when I get back I want you gone. Understand? I don't trust no professor's kid."

"Yessir! Gone, I'll definitely be gone!" Mr. Plucowski turned away and set off for the restroom. As he moved across the floor the crowd parted to let him pass. Nicky Neill had to work fast. He sidled closer to his friend. "Look, Ploox, I don't have a lot of time here, so listen up. You know about my dad being on that project down in Mexico, right?"

Ploox nodded.

"Well, he disappeared in the jungle three days ago. Vanished! No one has seen him since, no one has a clue where he might be."

"Oh." Ploox's expression remained blank, but his eyes narrowed to tiny slits. "The smoke in here's somethin' awful, ain't it?"

"Yeah, it's bad all right. Listen, I'm here because I'm running away from home. Now ... today. I'm going to Mexico to find Dad."

"Okay!" His eyes brightened. "Yer here to catch the bus, too. Maybe we can sit together?"

Nicky Neill shot another look toward the bathroom. Soon Mr. Plucowski would be out. "Ploox, I'm not taking the bus. I'm here for you."

"Me? Why me?"

"Because I need backup."

"Yuh mean like someone to stand behind ya?" he asked.

"Not behind me, Ploox, beside me! I need a traveling partner, someone who's strong and gutsy. You're my only choice."

"Huh? Huh!" His mouth flopped open. "Why duddn't yer mama go? Or what about takin' Phin as a partner?"

"No way, Ploox. You think I want my mom wandering around in a jungle full of jaguars and snakes? If anything happened to her we'd all be orphans. And you can forget about me taking my little brother down there. So what do you say?"

"Sorry Nicky Neill, but there ain't no way I can go with ya. Pop's buyin' muh ticket right now. I'm goin' ta Pawhuska, leavin' at ten till two fer the Institute." He relaxed and a satisfied smile spread over his face. "I reckon I'm gonna learn me a trade. And," he beamed proudly, "Papa says there'll be no flunkin' sixth grade a third time fer me. No, sir, a thirteen year old's gotta move on."

"No way, Ploox! You're not going to be on that 1:50 for Pawhuska, hear me? You don't belong at *The PIT*. You're a daydreamer, not a dummy. Come on; grab your bag. If you don't come with me now you'll never be free again."

"But, Nick ... muh Dad's right here. I cain't..."

"It's a prison, Ploox. The place is surrounded with barbed wire and they lock you in your room every night. You don't want to go there!"

"I don't care. I'm more scared o' muh Pop than that joint."

"But this is your chance to be a hero. If we rescue my dad even Josie Dobbs will want to be your friend." Nicky Neill hoisted Ploox's duffel bag off the floor and jammed it into his hands. "We've got to get out now!" He put a hand on his friend's back and gave him a sharp nudge towards the exit.

Before following after Ploox, Nicky Neill threw one last look at the bathroom doors. When he did, he locked eyes with Mr. Plucowski.

"Carpenter! You plant your butt right there!" Mr. P. plowed across the room, shaking a fist in Nicky Neill's direction. "Where's George? Where's my boy?"

"He's there, sir!" Nicky Neill pointed to the ticket window. "He's behind the counter! They're going through his bag! Uh, he's got too much stuff!"

"What the...?" Mr. Plucowski turned away and stormed towards the ticket agent. But he didn't forget about Nicky Neill. "You stay put, bub!" he shouted over his shoulder. By the time the echo of his command had died Nicky Neill was already through the door, snatching his bike away from the wall.

As he scrambled around the corner he spotted Ploox, standing on the loading dock, in plain view of the waiting area inside. "Jeepers!" he blurted. "Get on!"

"Where?"

"The seat! Get on the seat. I'll stand on the pedals. Hurry up!"

Ploox's mom had sewn shoulder straps on to his duffel bag. He slipped into it like a backpack and climbed aboard. He wrapped his arms around Nicky Neill's waist and they were off.

"Why yuh doin' this to me, Nicky Neill? If'n muh dad catches us we'll both wish we wuz never born."

"It's too late to worry about that now ... we're already gone. And loosen up with the death grip, huh? I need to be able to move if you want me to pedal."

"Oh, sure. You betcha. Say, whut in the heck wuz yer pop doin' down in Mexico anyhow?"

"Insects," Nicky Neill grunted. "He was studying insects."

"Insects? Ya mean bugs?"

"You know that, Ploox. My pop's a bug man. An entomologist."

"So, whut happened to him? D'yuh think a giant tarantula gobbled him up?"

"Very funny, Ploox. All I know is, he was studying bugs in some jungle down there and then ... poof ... he disappeared! My mom just got word this morning he was missing."

"So why don't the cops down there go lookin' fer him? It'd be a whole lot easier than you an' me ridin' this dang bike all the way ta Mexico."

"The police down there could care less about a college professor, Ploox. And don't worry about the bike. We're only headed for the edge of town. I've got something else in mind for us." Nicky Neill quit talking and focused on pedalling. Ploox was heavier than he'd imagined and whatever he had in his bag, it was solid, too.

"Hey!" Ploox suddenly piped up. "Is this gonna be an adventure?"

Nicky Neill decided not to mention the fact that Ploox's old man was already hot on their heels. "An adventure!" he gasped, straining to pedal and talk at the same time. "It's going to be an adventure, all right. Just hang on, partner. And don't look back."

CHAPTER 2

"**N**o, Ploox! Not in your mouth! In the air, like this." Nicky Neill held his fist to Ploox's face; thumb up.

"Oh! Okay! I gotcha now." Ploox's eyes brightened. "So this is whut they call hitchhikin', huh?"

"You got it. And we better get picked up fast before someone we know sees us."

Ploox frowned. "Like muh dad, right?"

Before Nicky Neill could respond, he noticed a car pulling out of Dooley's station, about a quarter mile away.

"Hey! Lookit, Ploox. Someone's headed our way. Maybe we'll get lucky this time."

As the car approached them it continued to pick up speed. Judging by the roar of the engine the driver had no intention of stopping. The boys looked on as their chance of escape sped past. Then the car's brake lights flashed on, followed by a squealing of rubber. They watched, wide-eyed, as a cloud of smoke and dust billowed up from the highway. When the air cleared they spotted the vehicle at rest on the gravel shoulder. A man's burly forearm shot through the driver's window, waving them over.

"Come on, Ploox! Grab your pack. Shake a leg before he changes his mind!"

"Yee-haw!" Ploox crowed with excitement. "We did it!"

When they reached the car, Nicky Neill poked his head through the window on the passenger's side. "Which way you headed, mister?"

A husky, sunburned man with a wide grin looked him over. "I'm Texas bound, sonny boy!"

"Great! So are we! Could we hitch a ride with you, sir?"

"Hell's bells, son! That's why I'm here! I'd love the company." He leaned towards the boy, pushed the door open and flipped the front seat forward. "Hop in!"

"Hey!" Ploox cried out over his friend's shoulder. "Can I ride shotgun?"

"You betcha, pardner!" The man's grin spread even wider. "Help yerself."

Nicky Neill tossed his pack into the back seat and climbed aboard. Just as he was getting settled Ploox's bag came crashing into his face, followed by a rude blow to his knees as his friend slammed the seat upright. The car lurched forward and began fishtailing down the shoulder of the highway with one of Ploox's legs still dangling out the open door. The instant he pulled it inside the heavy door slammed shut. A split second later they were on the highway, speeding south at a frightening clip.

"Waaah-hoo!" the driver sang out at the top of his lungs. Then he leaned across Ploox's lap and reopened and closed the door. "'Scuse me, biggun!" he laughed. "Wouldn't wanna lose ya now!"

The man returned to his position behind the wheel and paid momentary attention to his driving while he passed a slow-moving tractor. That accomplished, he looked over his shoulder in Nicky Neill's direction. "Just where, exactly, are you boys headed, anyhow?"

"Uh, we're headed for ..." Nicky Neill was about to tell him they were bound for Dallas to visit his uncle when Ploox interrupted him.

"We're runnin' away ta Mexico, mister! We're gonna find Nicky Neill's daddy!" Ploox twisted around in his seat and smiled proudly.

"Mexico, huh?" Their driver continued to look Nicky Neill over in the rearview as he spoke. "First time I run away from home I didn't plan on goin' no further than the pool hall 'crost town. Why Mexico?"

" 'Cause his daddy's gone missin', that's why," Ploox interrupted.

"You!" The stranger poked a finger in Nicky Neill's direction. "You tell me what you boys is all about."

Nicky Neill hesitated for a split second, and then decided to just tell him the truth. Besides, Ploox had already let the cat out of the bag. "Well, it's like he said. We're going to look for my dad. He disappeared in some jungle in Mexico a few days ago and the police down there don't seem to care."

"How you know 'bout all this?" The man's forehead wrinkled and a curious expression settled over his face.

"My mom, sir. She got word this morning. That's why we're running away."

"I don't follow ya, son." For a moment he pulled his eyes away from the mirror and glanced at the highway. Then his gaze came right back at Nicky Neill, waiting.

"My mother was going to go down there herself, leaving me, my little brother and my baby sister with our grandma. I couldn't let that happen. If something happened to my mom I'd never get over it."

"Yeah!" Ploox chimed in. "An' then they'd all be orphans and hafta go live in the poorhouse!"

"That's pretty much it, sir. That's why we're here." The two locked eyes in the rearview and for a second or two they studied each other. "You're not going to turn us in, are you, mister?"

"Let me see now, sonny boy. Y'all ain't nothin' but a couple o' kids ... and runaways at that. How old you say you was?"

"Twelve, sir," Nicky Neill replied.

"Not but twelve, huh? In my books that spells trouble with a capital T. You gotta understand I don't need no run-ins with the law."

"I know what you mean, mister, but you don't need to worry about us. I swear on a stack of Bibles we won't squeal on you. And besides, wouldn't you like to help a kid find his dad?"

The man glanced at the road then turned back to face Nicky Neill. "Well, if that don't beat all!" The smile returned to his face. "I like that, yessir! You boys got spunk!" He turned back around and slapped Ploox on the leg. "Welcome aboard! Leon Teeters is my name and the oil patch is my game. An' this here automobile is the Yella Hawk!" He flashed a toothy grin and gave the dashboard a loving pat. Then he poked a greasy thumb at Ploox. "What's yore name, hoss?"

"Uh, muh name's George, sir. But ever'one calls me Ploox."

"Then Ploox it is! Hmm, I like that name. Ploox!" He repeated it over and over, clearly enjoying the way it rolled off his tongue. "How 'bout you, bucko?" He shot Nicky Neill another glance through the rearview mirror.

"Nicky Neill, sir." His response was tentative. Something just didn't seem quite right. Mr. Teeters devoted more attention to his passengers than he did to the highway. And there was something else, too. A strange odor lingered in the air; one Nicky Neill couldn't quite put his finger on. Still, he shut up and stared out the window. Things weren't all bad. Not fifteen minutes after they had stuck out their thumbs they were heading south. If their luck held they'd be in Mexico in no time.

CHAPTER 3

"Whuttya do in the oil business, Mr. Teeters?" Ploox asked.

"Call me Leon, sonny." His perpetual grin widened. "I'm a driller. See them rigs yonder?" He pointed across a field towards a number of pumping units. "Them's the result o' my handy work. I'm good at what I do ... an' I draw a right fine wage, too. Heck fire, men! Ol' Leon's gonna buy hisself a bran' new set o' wheels once he gits to Abilene. An' ya know what sort o' ride I'm fixin' to purchase?"

"Naw," Ploox gasped. "Whut, Leon?"

"A pink Caddy, that's what! A 1958 Cadillac, with white-wall tires an' power steerin'. Yessir, the women love a pink Caddy! An' I do love the ladies!"

"Wow! Sounds swell," Ploox mumbled. Leon was about to say more, but he caught Nicky Neill's eye in the rearview mirror.

"Say, hoss. Ya mind fetchin' me one o' them brown trout outta the ice bucket? All this jawin' is makin' my throat scratchy."

Nicky Neill scanned his surroundings and spied a metal cooler on the floor behind Leon's seat. He popped the lid and pushed his hand through the ice until it made contact with an object.

"This it?" he asked, holding a long necked bottle above the seat for Leon's approval.

"Yep, that's her. Pass it up, champ."

Nicky Neill passed the cold glass into Leon's waiting hand and pushed the lid back onto the cooler. With practiced precision, Leon wedged the bottle between his legs and reached for a magnetized opener that clung to the dash. In one deft movement he popped the cap, flipping it onto the floor. The sound of escaping carbonation made a pleasant hissing noise. Leon returned the opener to its place on the dash and raised the bottle to his lips, slurping the bubbly foam.

"Aaah!" he sighed. "Thank ya kindly, sonny boy. That hits the ol' spot, dead center. *Burrrp!* Why, *ex-c-u-u-use* me!" At the sound of Leon's tumultuous belch Ploox erupted in laughter.

Leon took another long, satisfying swig. As he did he swerved into the opposite lane of the highway. At that moment it dawned on Nicky Neill that it wasn't pop their driver was swilling. It was booze, probably beer! His heart sank like a rock in shallow water. Their luck had turned out to be no luck at all. They were done for!

Ploox, on the other hand, was still clueless. For all he knew Leon's frosty brown bottle contained icy orange soda.

"Whutcha drinkin', Mr. Teeters? I mean, Leon."

Leon held the bottle aloft. "Why, this here's Kansas Kool-Aid, boy! Wanna give it a try?"

"Sure," Ploox chuckled, "I guess so."

"Hey, Nicky Neill! Fetch me another one o' them Kool-Aids, huh? An' while yer at it, snag one fer yerself. Hot diggity! I reckon we'll jus' have ourselves a little party!"

"Uh, no thanks, Leon. I'll stick with my canteen." Nicky Neill didn't want to test Leon's temper, so he did as he was asked and handed a fresh bottle forward, which Leon promptly opened and passed to Ploox. Nicky Neill sank back in his seat, not wanting to believe what was happening. He knew he had to come up with something to get them out of this jam.

Meanwhile, there was Ploox, perched in the front seat like the King of Siam. One elbow rested on the windowsill. In the opposite hand he clutched a cold bottle of beer. And he was swigging away on the stuff like he did it everyday! Nicky Neill thought about ordering Leon to stop the car and let them out. But Leon was partying and if he got mad there was no telling what he might do.

"How d'ya like it, Ploox?" Leon shouted.

"Great stuff, Leon ... once ya git used to it!" Ploox took another long pull at his bottle and then began to giggle. "Aaah!" he sighed. "An' it quenches muh thirst, too!"

"You betcha!" Leon sang out. "A Kool-Aid a day gits a man on his way! Ha-ha-ha!"

"Kansas Kool-Aid," Ploox murmured. "Wonder why Mama never brought any home fer us?"

"Excuse me, Leon," Nicky Neill interrupted as their new-found friend prepared to deliver another pearl of wisdom. "Why is it you call this car the Yellow Hawk? Is there a story behind that?"

"Story!" he cried. "You betcha there's a story behind that name!" He shot a knowing wink at Ploox. "This here's a '53 Chevy an' it's yeller as canned corn, huh? Am I right? It's the most yellowest car Chevrolet ever done made."

"Yes, sir," Nicky Neill echoed. "That's true, it's definitely yellow."

"Ah-hah!" Leon drained the contents from the bottle he was holding and flicked the empty container through the window. "Fetch me another, Snicky Sneel! An' be quick about it!" He glanced at Ploox. "An' a second round for my pal, George!"

"Yeah!" Ploox twisted in his seat. Both of them were shouting now when they spoke. "Another Kool-Aid fer George! An' be quick about it, Snicky Sneel!"

While Ploox reveled in his impersonation of Leon, Nicky Neill passed another round to the front seat. As he handed Ploox's bottle to him he shot his friend a nasty glare, but Ploox hardly noticed.

"Now, where wuz I?" Leon exclaimed. "Oh, yeah! The Yella Hawk!" He paused to hoist his bottle. "Okay! Okay!" he beamed. "She's yella, ya got that part. I tacked the Hawk on to the name because ..." he flashed an insane grin in the mirror "... because she can really fly! Yaaaa-hooooo!!" Leon's foot slammed against the gas pedal and the car lurched forward as if it had been shot from a cannon.

15

"Hey, Leon!" Ploox yelled above the engine's roar. "Whuddaya do with an empty bottle?"

"Pitch it!" he shouted back. "Pitch it high an' watch it fly!"

"Okay!" Ploox's head flopped up and down in loose agreement. "Here goes!" He poked his arm through the open window and hurled the bottle skyward. An instant later the empty came crashing down upon the hood, glass shattering everywhere.

"Yeeee-doggies, Ploox!" Leon wailed. "Bull's-eye!"

Nicky Neill slouched back in his seat. He had promised Ploox adventure all right, but he hadn't counted on things being so crazy. And he sure as heck hadn't planned on any action this soon! If they lived through this, he promised himself, he would be more careful in the future.

"A hunnert!" Leon crowed. "Lookit, Ploox! Lookit there! We're toppin' a hunnert miles an hour. Yeah! This is it, boys! This is livin'!"

CHAPTER 4

"*B*urrr-uppp!*" Ploox belched mightily and turned a bright crimson. But Nicky Neill could see he was proud of his accomplishment. It was a masterpiece of bad manners.

"Hey, Ploox! I'm impressed!" Leon had slowed the car down again, but only so his words could be heard. "You keep that up an' I'll get ya a job on the rigs when we pull into Texas. Hah-hah!" With that compliment a look of pure satisfaction settled over Ploox's face.

"Here goes another one, Leon!" Ploox lifted his second empty bottle and allowed Leon to inspect the corpse.

"Give 'er the ol' heave-ho, son!"

"Right, Cap'n! Bombs away!" With a lazy motion Ploox moved his arm towards the window. But, instead of clearing the opening, the bottle struck the frame and shattered inside the car.

"Eeeee-haaa! No cupie doll fer you, sonny! Watch this!" Leon stretched his arm out the window and made a mighty heave, sending the bottle sailing over the roof. They all watched as it crashed into the ditch and exploded on impact.

"Neat-o!" Ploox marvelled.

"You'll get the hang of it with practice." Leon twisted around in his seat to face Nicky Neill. "Two more Kool-Aids, Nickel Peel! If ya please!"

"Coming right up!" Nicky Neill shouted. As he dug into the chest he said to Leon, "Would you mind taking a peek at the road, Mr. Teeters?"

"Road?" he repeated, blankly. "Oh, THAT road! Sure thang." As Nicky Neill passed the bottles forward a huge semi-truck swerved onto the opposite shoulder to make room for them. The angry driver blasted his air horn, but it didn't faze Leon at all.

"Thank ya kindly, sonny," he mumbled, taking the bottles from the boy's hand.

"Yeah, ditto!" Ploox mimicked. "Thank yuh kindly, sonny!" Ploox was acting larger than life up front with his new-found friend. Nicky Neill shook his head in disgust. He was beginning to think he'd made a bad choice for a traveling partner.

"Hey!" Leon straightened up in his seat. "How 'bout we have ourselves a little sing-along? You like singin', Ploox?"

"Sure! Only nobody 'lows me ta sing at home."

"That does it then! We're singin'!" Leon grabbed up the opener on the dash and began to wave it like he was leading an orchestra. "Hank Williams, he's my man! We'll lead off with 'Hey, Good Lookin',' whaddya say?" He launched into the song without waiting for either one of the boys to join in. When he got to his favorite part he threw his head back and howled like a coyote. Nicky Neill leaned forward and squinted at the speedometer. They were doing ninety-five. Suddenly, the Yellow Hawk slipped across the center line into the path of an oncoming pickup truck.

"Watch out!" Nicky Neill screamed, grabbing Leon by the shoulder.

"Whoa-ooo!" Leon's eyes widened. He twisted the steering wheel violently, swinging them back into the right lane at the last minute. As he struggled to regain control of the car his beer shot out of his hand, emptying onto his lap. "Well, I'll be! We gotta pull over! I'm plumb soaked!"

A feeling of exhilaration swept through Nicky Neill. At last, they were stopping. They might live after all. He had to think fast. If they got back onto the highway with Leon their lives wouldn't be worth a plugged nickel.

CHAPTER 5

"Zippity-doo-dah!" Leon announced as they ground to a bumpy halt on the roadside. "It's time we made a pit stop anyhow. This'll give us a chance to irrigate some o' this here red Oklahoma dirt! Ha-ha-ha!"

"Boy howdy!" Ploox chimed in. "I wuz hopin' we'd stop. Them Kool-Aids go through yuh real fast!"

Leon killed the engine and they cleared the car. Nicky Neill plowed into the tall grass and headed towards the barbed wire fence that bordered a field of cut wheat. A short distance beyond the fence stood a cluster of pecan trees. He vaulted the fence and turned to wait for Ploox to catch up. They needed to talk if he was going to free them from Leon.

But Ploox and Leon were approaching together. They were a pathetic sight. The two of them were weaving and bobbing like a pair of staggered boxers. When Leon reached the fence he raised a leg to step over but lost his balance and fell backwards, tearing a huge slit in one pant leg. He cut loose with a stream of words that Nicky Neill had only heard around the bowling alley.

Ploox, meanwhile, was on all fours eyeballing the wire. After a moment he flopped to his belly and wriggled under the bottom strand like some giant bull snake. When he thought he was clear he looked at Nicky Neill and smiled. But he was not yet beyond the wire. When he attempted to rise up one of the barbs bit him on the butt.

"Yow! Owww-ch! That hurt!"

"Serves you right," Nicky Neill said, coming to help him to his feet. "Now listen up, we've go to ..." Before he could finish Leon swayed into sight and began herding them toward the pecan grove.

"Le's go, men! Texas ain't gittin' no closer with us standin' here. Do yer bizness an' reboard or I'm off without ya!"

"Sure thang, Leon!" Ploox pulled away and stumbled after his mentor. All Nicky Neill could do was watch after them. When they were finished they staggered back to the fence arm in arm. Nicky Neill continued to ogle them as they churned through the grass. Once they reached the car Ploox climbed into his shotgun position while Leon popped the trunk and grabbed a clean pair of jeans.

"Come on now, Neilly Nick!" Leon was standing beside the car in his underwear, a fresh pair of Levi's dangling from his hand. "Shake a leg, boy! Shake a leg!"

Nicky Neill hopped the fence and climbed back into the car. He figured if this was what fate had in store for him there was no avoiding it. As for Ploox, he'd read somewhere that people who were drunk were usually so relaxed they had a better chance of surviving a wreck than the average, non-intoxicated person.

CHAPTER 6

*B*ack in the car Leon spanked the dashboard before turning the key. With a rude jolt, they were off. They sped straight across the highway onto the far shoulder before Leon was able to gain control and bring the car back on course.

"Hey, now!" Leon sang out, reaching towards the radio. "How 'bout a few tunes?" With a twist of the knob there came a burst of static then a serious voice crackled over the speaker. All three of them leaned forward to listen.

"Urgent!" The announcer's voice was laced with dread. "I repeat: urgent! This is a news bulletin. We have an important message for all citizens of southern Oklahoma. Marvin, alias Cockeye, McGuffee, the notorious machine gun killer, has escaped from his cell at the state penitentiary in Millwood. Be on the lookout for this dangerous fugitive. He is extremely violent and may be armed. Call the nearest police unit in your area if you receive any information that might lead to his capture. We will keep you advised of the situation as it develops. Now, back to our regularly scheduled programming."

"Can you believe them apples! Ol' Cockeye done busted outta the pen! I never figgered they'd keep that boy behind bars fer long. Nobody'll be pickin' up hitchhikers now, fellas." The soothing voice of Patsy Cline drifted over the airwaves. It had a calming effect on them all. For the moment, at least, Leon stared at the road ahead.

"I think I'll take a nap," Nicky Neill said quietly. "If you guys don't mind?"

"Naw," Leon winked at him through the rearview mirror, "but how 'bout a couple more cold ones before ya git all tucked in!"

21

"Hey! I meant to tell you. You're out of Kool-Aids."

"Outta cold ones!" Leon slammed his fist against the dash and mumbled a few choice words. "Well, okay, then ... I guess that's that. Tough break, huh, Ploox?"

But Ploox barely mustered a reply. Something was happening to him. His complexion was beginning to take on a certain green appearance.

"What the heck. Reckon I'll jus' fire up a Lucky Strike an' count my blessings. You boys smoke?"

"No, sir! No thanks!" Nicky Neill answered. Ploox wasn't speaking. Instead, he was hugging the windowsill, gulping fresh air like a fish out of water.

Leon lit a cigarette and settled back into his role as driver. Nicky Neill pretended to be sleeping, but he kept his eyes open just enough to keep track of things. Five minutes passed. Leon flipped his cigarette butt out the window and began to fidget. Then he bolted upright.

"Hey! I can't be outta Kool-Aid! That kid's gotta be wrong!" Leon writhed around in his seat and jammed one hand down to the cooler. "Danged lid!" he exclaimed. "Fer cryin' out loud!" Then he brought his other arm around and attacked the ice chest with both hands.

"Leon!" Nicky Neill jumped up and attempted to help him. "Hold it, Leon! You drive, I'll do that!" But it was too late. With a dull, sickening, "KA-CHUNK ... KA-CHUNK," the two left tires popped off the concrete onto the shoulder of the wrong side of the highway.

"Whoa now, Nellie. Easy does it," Leon muttered. "Still got two tires on solid ground. I'll git us straightened out, pronto!"

But there was a four-inch ridge of concrete separating the soft shoulder from the highway. Leon hadn't figured on that. With a hefty twist of the wheel he hoped to bring all four tires back onto the road. Instead, the two left tires bit into the ridge and in one crazy, unforgettable instant, the Chevy flipped onto its roof and proceeded to skid along the ditch like a bullet over ice.

CHAPTER 7

*N*icky Neill had seen it coming. He had anticipated it. But he still wasn't prepared when the car flipped. In a split second the world turned upside down and he found himself clawing at the headliner with one of Ploox's oversized boots grinding its imprint into his forehead. The interior of the Chevy had been transformed into a free-fire missile range. Ice, beer bottles, backpacks, and pieces of broken glass whizzed through the air. Leon's sturdy metal cooler launched itself from the floor behind his seat and bashed him in the back of the head.

The Yellow Hawk continued to slide out of control until it crashed into something solid, flipped upright and came to an immediate halt. For a few seconds Nicky Neill remained pinned to the floorboard behind the front seat. Once he realized he was still alive he called out to the others. "Ploox! Leon!" His voice was shaky, uneven. "Are you guys all right? Talk to me!"

"Huhhh? ... Whut happ-ened?" From somewhere inside the car Ploox moaned. "Nicky Neill ... I can still talk. Whut's that mean?"

"It means you're still alive, that's what!" Nicky Neill pried himself from the floor and began inspecting his body for broken bones and other injuries.

"Whut about Leon?" Ploox grunted, attempting to hoist himself from beneath the dashboard.

"I don't know about him, except I can see he's bleeding." Nicky Neill stopped talking to sniff the air. "Oh, no! I smell gas! We've got to get out of here!" He eased himself through the shattered rear window and crawled around to Ploox's door. Their packs were lying on top of Leon, wedging him into place behind the steering wheel. "Pass me our bags, Ploox. Then get out, fast! We've got to get Leon clear of the car somehow. I think she's going to blow!"

Ploox was not his usual self. He was drunk and it showed. It took way too long for him to squirm free of the car. Outside, Nicky Neill looked him over. He was lucky too. Nothing broken. But he couldn't walk; he preferred to remain on all fours. Nicky Neill hustled around to Leon's door. As he moved he felt a sharp pain shoot up his left leg. At the same time he noticed a thin stream of blood running across his cheek. He wiped at it as he knelt beside the driver's window. "Mr. Teeters!" he yelled into Leon's ear. But their driver didn't respond. Nicky Neill was afraid he might be dead. He reached through the open window and lifted Leon's hand out. For a moment he held his breath, feeling for a pulse.

"Is he?" Ploox pressed close behind his partner. "Is he ..."

"I don't know. But we've got to hurry!" Nicky Neill began to tug at Leon's arm, trying to pull him through the window. "Come on, Ploox! Don't just sit there! Give me a hand!"

To Nicky Neill's astonishment, Ploox reached forward and lifted the door handle. All at once the door flew open and Leon spilled into his lap. "Well, I'll be doggoned!"

"Now whut? Aaagh!" Ploox gasped when he saw the blood covering the back of Leon's head.

"Take hold, we have to move him away from the car." Even though Leon was half out it was still a chore dragging him clear. "Keep pulling!" Nicky Neill wheezed. Suddenly, a small explosion erupted inside the car followed by a thunderous boom. Within seconds the Chevy was consumed in a ball of flame.

"Would yuh lookit that!" Ploox gawked, shielding his face from the heat.

"Yeah, I see it all right. And we could have been in there, too, frying like bacon." They continued to stare at the spectacle until Nicky Neill snapped to his senses. "Jeepers! What are we doing? Come on, Ploox! We've got to get out of here before someone spots us. Once the police show up there's going to be all kinds of questions ... questions we don't want to answer."

"But, whut about Leon?"

"Leon's alive and there's nothing more we can do for him. Besides, even though he looks bad, I don't think he's feeling much pain. The cops will call for an ambulance. He'll pull through." As Nicky Neill looked at Ploox he noticed his friend was beginning to turn a ghastly pale. "It looks like you're about to pay the price for all those Kool-Aids you drank."

"Yeah, I ain't feeling so hot ... like I'm about to puke or somethin'."

"You'll have to puke later, Ploox! Come on, let's scram! Make for those woods across the highway."

The boys grabbed their backpacks and sprinted over the concrete, disappearing into a thick patch of forest. When they were hidden they dropped to the ground and caught their breath.

"Sssh! Listen!" In the distance they could hear the sound of an approaching car. "Stay low," Nicky Neill warned, but Ploox was already as low as he could go. He was doubled up in a tight ball, puking his guts out. To escape the smell Nicky Neill crawled towards the highway where he had a better view of the wreck.

A light blue Oldsmobile rounded the curve and began to slow down at the sight of the accident. When the Olds stopped a young guy jumped out and raced over to Leon. Taking one look, he dashed back to his car and pulled a couple of blankets from the trunk. Without wasting any time, he spread one blanket over the unconscious victim and positioned the second one beneath Leon's head. Then he started pacing, trying to figure out what to do next. Just then, an old red Buick crept around the bend. The young guy ran towards the newcomer, waving his arms and jumping up and down.

"Ma'am! Ma'am!" he shouted to the older woman behind the wheel. "There's been a terrible accident here! I gotta go for help!" That was all Nicky Neill was able to hear. At that point the woman rolled her window down and their discussion became less audible. A minute passed. Nicky Neill watched the man pat the lady on the shoulder, spin away and run towards his car. Midway, he stopped and turned around. "No, ma'am!" he called back. "I promise you, he's still alive! He musta crawled out. I just hope there wasn't anyone in there with him!"

With those words hanging in the air he jumped into his car and sped off, leaving a long trail of burned rubber and smoke in his wake. In the space of a few seconds he disappeared down the ribbon of highway.

CHAPTER 8

For ten, maybe fifteen minutes, Nicky Neill crouched there, watching the Yellow Hawk burn. In that time the old woman kept her eye on Leon, but from a distance. It looked like she was afraid of being near a dead man. Ploox, meanwhile, had stopped being sick. He just lay there, moaning, writhing in the bushes from time to time like some terminally injured reptile. Then the wail of a siren pierced the stillness and a police car came speeding around the curve, followed by the blue Oldsmobile.

As the cars braked to a halt a husky patrolman stepped from his cruiser and surveyed the scene of the accident. Then, in a real take-charge style, he made his way to Leon's side. The young guy was right behind him.

The lawman knelt close to Leon's face. Several minutes later he stood up, returned to his car and began making notes on a clipboard. At one point he looked back at the scene of the accident and shook his head in disgust.

All of a sudden the young guy started shouting. The cop dropped what he was doing and raced back to the wreck. Again, the officer crouched beside Leon, but this time he put his ear close to the victim's face. After a few seconds he rose up and called out to the lady, "Ma'am! Did you see any boys 'round this accident?"

She shook her head no. Then, right out of the blue, her arms flew up in the air and she crumpled to the ground. The thought of a couple of kids roasting in that smoldering Chevy was too much for her. The men raced to her side. Not long after, another siren could be heard wailing in the distance. Soon an ambulance skidded onto the scene.

"Whudda we do now?" Nicky Neill turned to find Ploox at his shoulder, eyeballing the activity across the road. He looked awful, but the agony had disappeared from his expression.

"Welcome back," Nicky Neill whispered, holding a finger to his lips. "We stay put, that's what we do. At least, until it gets dark. I've got a feeling there's going to be more cops out here poking through the wreck ... looking for us!"

"Oooooh!" Ploox moaned long and low. "Why do I feel so sick? Am I hurt from the wreck?"

Nicky Neill started to let him have it, but Ploox was in so much misery he just couldn't do it. Poor guy, he was only having fun. He still didn't realize what had K.O.'d him.

"No, Ploox. You're not hurt." Nicky Neill put an arm around his friend's shoulder. "You're just sick. That Kansas Kool-Aid you chugged was really beer."

"Beer!" he cried. "Oh, golly! Am I gonna die?"

"No, you'll live." Nicky Neill took the canteen from his pack and offered it to his friend. "Here, wash your mouth out and clean yourself up." When Ploox finished he looked at his partner with a sheepish grin. The color was beginning to return to his face. "Listen to me, Ploox. You've got to learn to take care of yourself on this trip. I'm getting the feeling it's a crazy world out here. It's not like home. There's no one looking out for us but ourselves. And we have to be really careful with strangers. Remember, just because they're adults doesn't mean we can trust them. Understand?"

"Yeah, I'll be careful. But Leon was such a nice guy. Ooh, muh head! I'm sleepy. Why am I so sleepy?"

"Go on, roll over and have a nap. We're not going anywhere for awhile."

Ploox collapsed on his bag and passed out. Nicky Neill sat there watching him. "Yeah, big guy," he whispered, "catch some Z's. You'll feel better when you wake up. Maybe by that time we'll be able to get moving again."

CHAPTER 9

While Ploox slept, Nicky Neill kept an eye on the action across the road. Not long after the ambulance departed a whole slew of new faces arrived. Rows of vehicles lined both sides of the road. Before long a couple of policemen had to station themselves on the highway to direct traffic.

As safe as Nicky Neill thought they were, there came a time late that afternoon when he figured their gooses were cooked. It happened when the cop in charge organized a search party. Police and spectators alike joined up and began sweeping the area near the accident. Panic set in when the mob crossed the highway and and started beating the bushes in front of the boys. Nicky Neill began concocting tall stories about who they were and what they were doing there. But then some passer-by, gawking at all the commotion, ran his truck into one of the police cars. Nobody was hurt but everyone stopped searching and hustled back to the highway to watch the poor guy get his butt chewed. After that the manhunt was called off.

As the sun began to sink, a lone policeman supervised the towing away of the Yellow Hawk. Then the officer climbed into his car and drove off.

"Ploox! Ploox! Wake up, they're gone!" Nicky Neill gave his partner a couple of shakes.

"Wuz I dreamin'? Or wuz there really a big wreck?"

"You weren't dreamin', man! There was a wreck all right. And you've got a nice shiner to prove it." Ploox poked at his cheeks and winced when his fingers pressed the bruise below his left eye.

"Ow! That hurts. I ain't never had no black eye before."

"Well, you've got one now. Too bad I don't have a steak to slap on it!"

"A steak!" Ploox's whole face lit up. "Oh, man, Nicky Neill, I'm starvin'! An' I'm real thirsty, too."

"Yeah, me too."

"Hey!" Ploox began groping frantically in the brush. "Mom packed some o' muh favorite food in that duffel bag. Where's muh stuff?"

"Here, I've got it. Keep your voice down and I'll go through your gear for you." Nicky Neill dragged Ploox's bag over and opened it up. Right away a sharp odor pierced his nostrils. "Whew! Supper's ready!"

The boys dined on rank sausage and cheese and washed it down with lukewarm water. If those lawmen had come back with bloodhounds, poodles even, they would have been a cinch to track. By the time they finished their meal darkness had settled in. It was their cue to move on. As they slogged through the underbrush towards the highway Nicky Neill couldn't help but hope their luck had changed. Traveling by night seemed strange, but somehow it felt much, much safer.

CHAPTER 10

"Now whut?" Ploox stopped by the roadside to catch his breath. "Which way?"

"South, of course! We'll stay close to the ditch and just follow the highway. Sooner or later we're bound to hit a town. When we do, we'll figure something out. You ready to hike?"

Ploox peered up and down the empty strip of concrete, sniffing the clean night air as he pondered their situation. "Yep! I'm ready. I think I'm gonna like this part."

Five minutes into their march a pair of headlights popped over a rise in front of them. "Yikes! Hit the dirt!" Nicky Neill cried.

"Eeee-yuk!" Ploox squealed once the car had passed. "That was fun! I like divin' in the dirt!"

"Yeah," Nicky Neill smiled, dusting himself off. ""From now on, Ploox, we're with the Rat Patrol, sneaking around deep in Nazi territory. Can you handle it?"

"Why, sure!" He snapped to attention. "Call me Corporal Ploox! Ain't nobody gonna nab Corporal Ploox!"

From then on they acted like trained commandos, diving to the ground at the first hint of an approaching vehicle. They no longer traipsed beside the ditch; they swaggered in it. To top it off, Ploox started calling Nicky Neill "Sarge" whenever he spoke to him.

Several hours down the road they caught a glimpse of stationary lights twinkling in the distance.

"Zat a town, Sarge?" Ploox whispered excitedly.

"No, I don't think so. It's not big enough. Might be a truck stop or something. Keep your eyes peeled and we'll find out soon enough."

The boys prowled along the ditch at a quickened pace. Before long they were close enough to make out their objective.

"Hey, Nicky Neill! That's some kinda café ... an' a gas station, too!"

"Yeah, I know where we are now. We drive by this place every time we visit Grandpa and Grandma Carpenter. It's called the Broken Wheel."

"So," Ploox rubbed his hands in anticipation, "we goin' in fer a sodie pop an' a chicken fried steak?"

"Are you crazy? Why do you think we've been eating dirt all this way? Don't even think about going in there."

"But ... but ... whut then? We gonna walk all the way to Mexico? An' I'm hungry again!"

Before Nicky Neill could answer his partner a rickety hay truck pulled off the highway and rolled to a stop beside the gas pumps. The boys watched as a man in overalls climbed from the cab and ambled towards the restaurant.

"That's it!" Nicky Neill whispered. "That's our ticket out of here!"

"Huh?" Ploox looked closer. "I don't see no ticket!"

"Listen! That old guy who just went inside, I know who he is. He's Old Man Cundiff from Tishomingo. He sells hay. My grandparents live in Tishomingo."

"So? Ya gonna buy some hay?"

"No, man! I mean Tishomingo is due south of here. Old Man Cundiff must be on his way home. All we've got to do is jump on board and ride the rest of the way. Before he reaches town we bail out. Come morning it's just a skip and a jump to Texas. And after Texas is Mexico!"

"Neat-o! I getcha now! C'mon, le's hop in the back." Ploox started to climb out of the ditch when the restaurant door slammed shut. The boys stared, mortified, as a man proceeded to switch on the gas pump and fill Mr. Cundiff's tank. At that moment Mr. Cundiff himself stepped from the building. He visited with the attendant for a minute then walked to the front of the truck and raised the hood. Soon, the other man joined him. One of the pair produced a flashlight and held it to the engine while the other stooped to make a close-up inspection. The lighting was poor where the two men conferred, making it hard to see what was going on.

"Oh, swell!" Ploox cursed. "So much fer our ride outta here!"

"No, we can still do it. But we have to move fast. Are you up for it?"

"But they'll see us, Nicky Neill! They'll catch us an' turn us in to the law!"

"Knock it off, Ploox! We're not criminals you know. Just runaways. Look, we are the Rat Patrol, right?"

Ploox nodded anxiously.

"Okay, then. Here's the plan. We make a run for it, to the back of the truck. While they're up front we hop on board, scoot into the shadows, and bingo! We're all set." Nicky Neill was about to sprint across the highway when Ploox grabbed his shirttail and pulled him back. "What! What now?"

"I don't know, Nicky Neill. I figure we better stay low so's the enemy don't see us. Wouldn't wanna git picked off by no machine gun fire now would we?"

"Good thinking. Now let's go. Follow me!"

Nicky Neill launched himself to the lip of the ditch and then darted across the deserted highway. Seconds later he was at the back of the truck, shoving his pack on board. Before he mounted up he squinted into the darkness along the roadside. He couldn't see his partner, but he could hear his big feet slapping against the concrete. Then he was there, rounding the line of gas pumps. It looked like he was home free before he slipped in the gravel and went down headfirst, sliding beneath Nicky Neill like a runner stealing home. There was a dull thud as Ploox's head collided with the right rear tire.

"Ummmfffttt!" he moaned. "I made it!"

"Good night, man! That was one heck of a slide. Let me give you a hand before those guys figure out we're here." Nicky

Neill pulled his partner to his feet, boosted him onto the truck and hopped in after him. Then the hood slammed shut and the attendant returned to finish his job at the pump. From the shadows, Ploox's whisper caught Nicky Neill's ear.

"Whut wuz that?"

Nicky Neill crawled up beside him. "I think we're leaving," he whispered. "Keep quiet!"

"Whut's the damage, Bill?"

"Six and a dime, Mr. Cundiff. You want I put that on a ticket?"

"Yeah, Bill, you do that. I'll catch ya in a day or two. So long now." Mr. Cundiff climbed into the cab and switched on the ignition. The engine sputtered to life. In a fit of shimmy and shake the old hay truck labored out of the station and onto the highway.

With the wind whistling through the railings Nicky Neill finally relaxed. They were off once again! Looking overhead, he gazed at an endless sea of stars twinkling away. It felt good to be alive and on the move, heading south towards Texas ... and then Mexico. "Hang on, Dad," he said softly, his words trailing into the breeze. "Hang on. We're on our way."

CHAPTER 11

*T*he lights of the Broken Wheel disappeared from view as Old Man Cundiff's rickety hay truck nosed into a wide, downward turn. Using his backpack for a pillow, Nicky Neill propped it behind his head and settled back to enjoy the ride.

"Hey!" Ploox wriggled in beside him. "Lookit that sky! Ain't that somethin' ... there mus' be a jillion stars up there."

"Yeah. Makes you feel pretty small, huh?"

"Uh-huh. But glad to be alive. Ya know whut I mean? An' ya know whut else?"

"No, Ploox. What?"

"I got little bitty goose bumps all over me jus' thinkin' 'bout our time with Leon. We coulda died in that wreck, ya know. Easy. But here we are, still alive ... still goin'. Thinkin' 'bout it makes me feel funny inside."

"I know what you mean. We had a brush with the Grim Reaper. One second we were busy living and breathing, and then WHAM! It was nearly lights out. It's scary, real scary."

After that the boys rode along in silence. Eventually, Ploox's curiosity got the best of him.

"Whut happens next? Ya think we can git this guy to drive us ta Mexico?"

"Are you kidding!" Nicky Neill laughed. "Old Man Cundiff would probably kick our butts if he caught us back here. But I do have a plan."

"Yuh do?" Ploox rolled to his side. "Whut is it?"

"A couple miles this side of Tishomingo there's a four way stop. When Mr. Cundiff slows down you and me are bailing out. Across the road is a huge wilderness, a game refuge. Once we're clear of the truck all we have to do is hike into the woods and find a camping spot."

"Wow! I ain't never camped out before."

"Well, you're going to tonight. And I know where there's a swimming hole in those woods. An early morning dip would be great, wouldn't it? Then Mexico, here we come!"

"Wow, sounds swell. Ya know, I think I'm glad I came on this trip. An' I been thinkin' 'bout somethin' else too."

"What's that, Ploox?"

"I been thinkin' 'bout how most dads in town won't even let me come in the house. But not your pop. He invites me in and sometimes even lets me stay for supper."

"Yeah, he's a pretty great guy all right. I just hope it doesn't take us too long to find him."

"Don't worry, Nicky Neill. If a car crash couldn't stop us ain't nothin' else gonna do it." With that Ploox rolled onto his back and returned to stargazing.

Before long, a rude grinding of gears signaled they were slowing down. "Time to move out, Ploox!" Nicky Neill nudged his friend in the ribs and began edging towards the front of the bed.

As the truck shuddered to a halt the boys jumped clear of the rig and hit the ground running. Well, almost anyway. Ploox struck the concrete on two feet but his momentum carried him to the edge of the road where he tripped and tumbled head over heels into a drainage ditch. By the time Nicky Neill found him, Old Man Cundiff and his hay wagon were nothing more than a vague pair of taillights disappearing in the distance.

CHAPTER 12

*O*nce Ploox got back on his feet the boys scampered up the small rise that led to the boundary of the game preserve. At the fence line they scanned the highway a final time before tackling the forest.

"Whew!" Ploox sighed. "Shore is dark out here all of a sudden! I cain't see nothin'." He was right. The heavens above twinkled and glowed like a great city at a distance, but on the ground the darkness was almost smothering.

"No sweat, pal." Nicky Neill tried to sound confident. "Once we make it into the woods I'll dig out my flashlight."

In short order the boys were wading through heavy forest. To Nicky Neill's dismay, the timber turned out to be nearly impenetrable. After several minutes of struggling with the underbrush they stopped to locate the flashlight.

"Man!" Nicky Neill mumbled, digging through his pack. "This is a jungle! It feels like we bailed out of Oklahoma and landed in Africa! Ah, here it is." He drew out his flashlight and switched it on, sweeping the area in all directions.

"Oh, m'gosh! This's impossible ... an scary, too! We cain't see nothin'! Oh, man!" Ploox crowded against his friend.

"What? What is it now?"

"If this is a game refuge then that means there's all kinds o' critters in these woods. Whut if a mountain lion or a grizzly bear hears us comin'? An' whut about snakes ... an' bats ... an' wild pigs? I heard some o' them pigs're big enough to track a man down an' eat 'im!"

"Ploox! Come on, relax! There are no lions or bears in here. Besides, most animals are more afraid of us. So don't worry, okay?"

"All right," he swallowed. "But you go first."

As Nicky Neill started off he felt his friend's hand take hold of his shirttail. But before he could take a second step, Ploox jerked him backwards. "Huh! Now what is it? Did you hear something?"

"I ... I jus' thought o' somethin' awful." Ploox's hand was trembling. "There could be someone in these woods a whole lot worse'n any animal. That convict could be hidin' out in here! You know, Cockeyed McGuffee. He wouldn't think nothin' o' killin' a couple o' kids!"

"Cockeye, Ploox! The guy's name is Cockeye. And believe me, the last place he's going to be is in these woods." Nicky Neill was doing his best to sound brave. "Hey," he continued, "look around. Even if the guy was in here, do you really think he could see us in this jungle? No way! And I bet if he was right under our noses he wouldn't make a peep. But just to be sure, no more talking until we find a trail or a campsite. Let's go!"

Nicky Neill kept the flashlight low to the ground as they continued to wind their way deeper into the brooding forest. But even with the light it was rough going. It felt like the forest itself had come to life and was determined to swallow them up.

The boys fought on until they stumbled into a clearing. "Ploox! Look at this! We made it! This is a perfect place to camp. We can roll out our blankets and sleep right here. What do you think?"

"Yeah! Looks okay to me. Whut's that over there?"

Nicky Neill focused the beam on a dark clump in the center of the clearing. It was a fire pit. A ring of blackened stones encircled a mound of charred wood and ashes. Several tree stumps stood nearby, drawn up to serve as stools.

"Hmm. Looks like someone else has used this campsite. But it's been awhile. Anyway, there's no sign of them now. Come on, Ploox! This place is ours."

"I dunno," he said, backing away from the center of the clearing. "This could be Cockeyed McGruder's hideout ... this could be where all them escaped convicts come to."

"Aw, knock it off, Ploox! Look around. There hasn't been a fire in that pit forever. Now come on, take your blanket out and let's get some shuteye. I'm too tired and sore to argue with you now." Nicky Neill proceeded to spread his blanket and arrange his gear.

"Oh ... well ... maybe. But do ya think we could leave the light on?"

"The flashlight? No way! We've got to make the batteries last."

"Well ... how 'bout a little fire then? Couldn't we jus' make a tiny li'l ol' fire? Please?"

"Ploox, are you afraid of the dark?"

"Well, I ain't never slept outside before."

"Oh, my gosh!" All Nicky Neill wanted was to put his head down and sleep. "Sure, Ploox. Make a fire if it'll make you feel better. But promise me you'll keep it small. No bonfire, okay?"

"Okay! I'll keep it small. Cross muh heart."

That was it for Nicky Neill. He flopped onto his blanket and shaped his jacket into a pillow. By the time his eyes slammed shut he was already asleep.

Sometime later, intense heat and a near-blinding light prompted Nicky Neill to bolt upright on his blanket. He opened his eyes to discover Ploox perched on one of the stumps. He was feeding a long limb into a fire that had become a raging blaze while mumbling to himself, "Gotta keep 'er goin'. Don't want no bogeymen comin' 'round here. Oh, Mama, help me, help me!"

"Ploox!" Nicky Neill shrieked. "What in the heck are you doing? I told you, no bonfire! You're going to burn the whole forest down! All they'd find of us would be a couple of toasted skeletons. Scatter that fire; let it burn out. Now!"

"Sorry, I'll make it little again. It's jus', I ain't tired on account o' muh nap this afternoon. Go back to sleep, Nicky Neill. I'll watch it close, honest."

"All right, you do that. But remember, no one can outrun a forest fire." Nicky Neill collapsed back onto his bedroll. As he was about to re-cross that bridge from consciousness to sleep, a booming, ominous voice called out from beyond the clearing's edge.

"Hey! What are you boys doing out there?"

CHAPTER 13

*T*he voice from the darkness echoed in the clearing like a burst of cannon fire. Nicky Neill was so frightened he became paralyzed. As for Ploox, he threw his hands above his head and pleaded in a high, cracking voice, "Don't shoot!"

"Stay right where you are," the voice commanded. "I'm comin' in."

Nicky Neill remained pinned to the forest floor. A split second passed. He managed to wriggle his toes, then his fingers. He could move again! If he could just gather his wits he might make a break for it. But what if the voice belonged to Cockeye McGuffee? He'd have a gun for sure, which meant he'd probably cut him down before he got clear of his blanket. And what about Ploox? Even if he was able to make an escape he couldn't leave his partner behind.

Before Nicky Neill was able to entertain any further notions he heard the forest floor giving away beneath the weight of heavy feet. This was it; the stranger was coming in behind him. In a heartbeat Nicky Neill decided not to take a bullet in the back. Instead, he flung the blanket off his shoulder and rolled over to face their attacker.

Then, just like that, he was there beside the campfire, looking at the boys as if he couldn't believe what his own eyes were seeing. Nicky Neill looked him over from head to toe and back again. The shoes on his feet were nothing more than ragged leather boats. Dark, well-worn trousers hung from his waist, cinched around an ample belly by a frayed length of twine. His pants were littered with patches and the jacket he wore was so wrinkled it was hard to identify as the top half of the corduroy suit it had once been. He supported a hefty stick across his shoulder. One end of the stick was fastened to a large burlap bundle.

"Well," the man said, nonchalantly, "do I need an invitation to join your campfire?"

CHAPTER 14

"No! No! I mean, please!" Nicky Neill sputtered. He sprang from his blanket. "Sit down, sir. Make yourself at home."

"That's more like it, my friend. But first, how about your buddy there drops his hands." He pointed towards Ploox, still seated in front of the fire. "This isn't a stick-up, you know? And get him to open his eyes, I'm not all that hard to look at!"

Ploox lowered his arms to his side. Gradually, he opened first one eye then the other. Seconds passed. "Are you ... are you Freddy the Freeloader?" he asked.

Nicky Neill cringed and looked to their visitor to gauge his reaction. At first there was none. He slumped one shoulder and allowed his stick and bundle to tumble at his feet. Then, in one supple motion, he collapsed to the ground as if it were a familiar easy chair waiting to cushion his fall. He tilted his hat away from his forehead, all the while looking right at Ploox. Then he began to laugh.

"Har-har-har! Har-har-har!" His laughter echoed through the clearing like the hoarse barking of some giant bear. "Freddy the Freeloader! Son, you've got a sense of humor! That's exactly who I am, only the name's not Fred. I'm Herb; Herb Fenugreek, man of the world, king of the road. I'm free as the wind, rich as fresh cream, and happy as a chipmunk on the first day of spring!"

Listening to him Nicky Neill began to relax. His voice was deep, comforting somehow. He spread his arms and continued talking. "This is my living room you're sprawled in, and these woods are just one of my many far-flung palaces. And you know what? I'm plumb tickled to have you boys here. Yessiree, you look like the best of company!"

By the time Herb finished his spiel Nicky Neill had taken a seat beside Ploox. The boys remained speechless, overcome by a peculiar captivation. Never, in their short lives, had they ever run across an adult like this one. With his hat tilted back, in the glow of the campfire, his face became visible. His eyes were a brilliant blue and they twinkled as he spoke through barely visible lips. A thick, curly beard merged with a great, unkempt head of matted hair. If Nicky Neill hadn't known better he would have sworn he was Santa Claus disguised as a bum.

"Now!" Herb leaned towards them, grinning from ear to ear. "What are you fellas doing out here, anyway?"

"Mr. Fenugreek," Nicky Neill began, "we're..."

"Herb," he interrupted. "My name's Herb."

"Sorry, sir. I mean, Herb. We're looking for my father."

He bolted upright. "Your father! Good golly, boy, is he lost? Is he in these woods?"

"Oh, no sir. He's lost down in Mexico. We're on our way to find him." Nicky Neill stopped talking when Herb slapped his knee and began stroking his beard.

"Well, color me pink, son!" he said at length. "Mexico, huh? You boys have some traveling ahead of you. What are you doing for transportation?"

"We hitchhiked today," Nicky Neill said with a note of pride. "But I don't think we'll be hitching again."

"Well, well, well." Herb clasped his knees and began rocking to and fro. "You guys are regular Marco Polos. I presume you had to run away from home to get here?"

"Yes, sir," Nicky Neill replied. He started to spill his guts, but Herb waved him to stop.

"Hold on, little brother. We all close the door on home sweet home some time. Some sooner than others. Once it's done, it's done. Now you're on the road; it's a new life for the both of you."

"It's not forever, Herb. Once we find my dad we'll go back home. We're still kids, you know."

Herb looked long and hard at Nicky Neill. The twinkle disappeared from his eyes. "Once you leave you can't ever go back," he said. "You can't go home again. Ever. Kids or not." He looked away from the boys and stared into the fire. Several long, uncomfortable minutes passed. Then he spoke up again. "Forgive my lack of manners, boys. You haven't told me your names yet."

"I'm Nicky Neill Carpenter."

"And I'm George Plucowski. But ever'one calls me Ploox."

"Well, Nicky Neill and Ploox," the glow returned to Herb's face and the warmth crept back into his voice, "it's late and we all need our beauty rest. Tomorrow I'll see what I can do about teaching you the game of survival ... hobo style. Sleep tight, lads."

Without further ado Herb flipped onto his back and pulled his satchel beneath his head. The boys looked on, dumbfounded, as their guest appeared to lapse into sleep. But then his eyes popped open and he wagged a finger in Ploox's direction. "And you, Ploox! Let that fire die out. I can't rest easy if I have to worry about being roasted alive!"

CHAPTER 15

*D*awn crept into the forest like a great, slow-moving river of glowing light. From where Nicky Neill lay in his blanket cocoon, the arrival of day did not seem real. He felt like an uninvited guest, peeking at the creation of the world. Then the rude thumping of heavy feet crashing through the underbrush destroyed his reverie. He rose up on one elbow and scouted the bush for the source of the commotion. Herb pulled himself up as well, startled by the same racket.

"What's out there, Herb?" Nicky Neill asked.

"Got me. But whoever or whatever it is, it's got big feet!" At that they both twisted around for a view of Ploox's bedroll. They laughed at the sight of his empty blanket. "Mother Nature came calling early!" Herb chuckled. "Time to get a move on anyway; sleeping in isn't part of life on the road."

"Mornin'!" Ploox sang out as he ambled into camp. "These woods ain't nearly so scary when ya can see where yer goin'. Hey! Whut's fer breakfast?"

"Well, now!" Herb began to beam. "Ploox, you're a man of my own making. What do you boys have on you in the way of grub?"

"Sausage and cheese," Nicky Neill answered, reaching for Ploox's backpack. "And we have plenty for you, Herb."

"Fine, that's just fine. And I've got a little something to contribute as well." The boys watched while Herb undid the knot on his burlap bag and began probing its contents. "Voila!" he sang out, lowering a wad of newspaper to his lap. With great care he pulled the paper apart and revealed three large, brown eggs. "And here," he grinned, shaking open a rumpled paper sack, "is our morning toast!" A half loaf of homemade bread tumbled out. "A kind lady by the name of Gladys gave me these things in exchange for a box of well-split kindling. Strap on your appetites, gents, because ol' Herb's going to put together a hobo omelette the likes of which you won't soon forget!"

Nicky Neill built a fire and soon the kitchen was in operation. The boys looked on in awe as Herb went to work. He toasted the bread over a framework of green sticks and cooked a sausage and cheese omelette in a coffee can he carried in his bag. While the omelette gurgled and sizzled he carved out three crude forks from the remnants of kindling the boys had gathered for the fire. When the meal was ready he folded sheets of newspaper into flimsy plates and they proceeded to dine like royalty. Between bites Ploox and Nicky Neill attempted to learn more about their newfound friend.

"Herb?" Ploox was the first to speak up. "Have you always been a hobo?"

Herb stopped chewing for a minute and cocked his head towards the smoldering fire. "No, Ploox," he sighed, "I haven't always been a hobo. I was a kid once myself you know, just like you." He began to chew his food again. "Then I grew up. I fell in love, got married, found a job. And there I was, set for life. Or so it seemed."

"What happened?" asked Nicky Neill.

"One day I looked in the mirror ... and the man staring back at me was a stranger." Like the night before, the glow faded from Herb's face. "Something inside of me changed at that moment."

"Well, whut?" Ploox chewed nervously, awaiting Herb's reply.

"I dropped my razor in the sink. My wife was still in bed. I watched her sleep for a minute or two, then I walked out the door and never went back. I've been on the road ever since, been nothing but a hobo."

Like Nicky Neill, Ploox was dumbstruck. Herb continued eating, but the boys could only sit there, unable to contemplate anything else except the image of his wife wondering what in the world had ever become of her husband.

"You ... you ..." Nicky Neill tried at last to say something, to clear the air, but his thoughts wouldn't gel. Instead, Herb settled it for him.

"I deserted my wife. That's what I did. I guess you could say I walked out on my life. I am a hobo, fellas. You got that?"

The boys nodded their acknowledgement.

"I'm not a mean person; I'm not evil. I regret the pain I must have put that woman through. But I did what I had to do. We live in a world of choices. I made mine." Then Herb looked at Ploox and Nicky Neill. A wry grin spread across his bearded face. "You, too, made a choice, boys. For better or worse, here you be." Another silence settled over the trio. This time Herb broke the spell. "I've got just one question for you two." His eyes began to twinkle again.

"Yes, sir?" Nicky Neill asked. "What is it?"

"You boys want to know where I'm bound?"

"Yeah!" Ploox crowed. "I wanna know!"

"I'm Texas bound," he said, pitching his plate onto the bed of glowing coals. "San Antonio, in fact. And unless I'm mistaken that's on the way to Mexico. You're welcome to tag along if you like."

"Yer gonna let us tag along! Hotdog! Man, that'll be swell, Herb." But Ploox noticed his partner was not so quick to commit. "Hey, Nicky Neill ... whut's wrong? Ain't ya glad Herb's lettin' us go with 'im?"

"Well, yeah," Nicky Neill stammered. "But we can't afford to wander around the countryside, if you know what I mean? No offense, Herb, but we're on a pretty urgent mission."

"I see," he smiled. "You're worried we'll take our sweet time moving south, huh? Well, let me tell you, I'm on my own private schedule. And I haven't got any time to waste myself."

"But how, then?" Nicky Neill interrupted. "Are you planning to walk the whole way?"

"Walk!" Herb feigned insult. "My young friend, travel is a hobo's stock in trade. You are looking at the master of the art of come and go." His gaze narrowed. "Rule number one, life on the road: never walk anywhere when you can just as easily hop a freight!"

CHAPTER 16

*P*loox never did get to swim that morning. But, with Herb in the picture, he was more eager than ever to get started. An exciting twist had been added to the adventure and a bright new day was flooding over the horizon.

Herb extinguished the campfire and helped the boys police the clearing. By the time they were ready to leave the place looked as if they had never been there. Hobo courtesy, he called it.

"Where to now?" Nicky Neill asked. He watched as Herb strapped his bundle to his shoulder stick.

"We're bound for Mill Creek, boys, a peaceful berg not far from here. I've got a special friend there who can see us off to Texas."

"A town!" Nicky Neill gasped. "What about the highway? Ploox and I can't afford to be out in the open."

"That's true. The two of you are probably wanted men by now. Lucky for you, then, we have no need of the highway. Just keep pace with old Herb and put your worries to rest." That said, he took off across the clearing and plowed into the forest. The boys followed in hot pursuit.

They crashed through thick brush for several hundred yards before Herb led them up a steep bluff and onto a narrow trail. After an hour of steady walking they broke out of the woods and found themselves staring at a span of railroad track.

"Now here," Herb said, peering down the rails, "is a highway you can live with. The rest of our little jaunt will be a cakewalk, I guarantee."

But hiking over the rail bed wasn't all that simple. Ploox and Nicky Neill stumbled repeatedly on the crossties until

Herb showed them how to establish a rhythm. After that it became a pleasant march.

Eventually, Ploox felt like talking. "Herb," he called out, "is a bum the same thing as a hobo?"

"Ploox!" Nicky Neill scolded.

"That's all right, son," Herb reassured him, "no offense taken. See here, Ploox," he continued, "there's a world of difference in what you just said. I'm not a bum. I'm all hobo. In my society there's four classes of citizen. First you've got your hobo, as in yours truly! We hobos are not afraid of hard labor; we just don't tolerate being tied down for long. Picking fruit, chopping wood, pitching bales, pushing a broom even ... I've done them all and that's how I keep going. Anyway, a hobo's free to move when he chooses." He paused to clear his throat. "Now, the next character down the rung is the tramp. He prefers life on the road, just like a hobo, only he doesn't care to work. That's the difference. He'll beg, borrow, maybe steal if he has to, but he sure as the devil won't work up a sweat to earn an honest dollar. It's the tramp who makes things tough for us hobos. And in the city it's the bum who spoils the lot. Understand, a bum is just a tramp only he's too lazy to get out and about. His thing is to hang around one spot and beg for money. Last, and no doubt least, is the wino. A wino is too far down the alcohol trail to do anything useful; all he cares about is where his next bottle is coming from. Avoid the tramp, the bum, and the wino, boys. They only bring trouble."

"Goll-eee," Ploox puffed, straining to keep up with Herb, "I didn't know nothin' 'bout them kinds o' people."

"Like I told you, fellas, life is about choices. Everybody makes them; some make better choices than others." Herb stopped walking and turned to face the boys. "Use your heads, lads. Sometimes one slip-up is all you get." Before they could respond he spun about and set off down the track again at the same brisk pace he had maintained from the start.

Except for the occasional water break they walked through the morning and into the afternoon. Nicky Neill's legs began to ache but he wasn't about to complain. Ploox, however, wasn't shy about letting his feelings be known.

"Whew!" he panted. "Are we gonna hike all the way ta San Antonio?"

"Hah! Take heart, my friend," Herb answered over his shoulder. "Mill Creek is just around the bend. When we arrive we'll look up Mr. John O'Brien. He'll have us rolling towards Alamo City in no time!"

"This Mr. O'Brien," Ploox huffed, "he got a car he'll loan us?"

"Does he have a car?" Herb allowed Ploox to draw alongside him. "Ploox, Johnny O'Brien *is* a car! A boxcar, that is. And come Mill Creek the three of us will board the six-oh-five for Dallas."

"Really?" Ploox was beaming. "No kiddin', Herb? Ya mean we're gonna hop a freight train? Tonight?"

"Indeed, my friend! Just like real hobos. In fact, this trip will qualify you both as Gay Cats."

"What's that?" Nicky Neill joined in. "I'm not so sure I want to be any kind of cat."

"Relax!" Herb stroked his beard and laughed as if he were remembering something long forgotten. "A Gay Cat is just another name for a beginning hobo. That's all."

With that news their pace quickened. Naturally, Ploox meowed the rest of the way into Mill Creek.

CHAPTER 17

*T*he trio reached Mill Creek in mid-afternoon. Like most places with rail service, the tracks ran along the outskirts of town. It was a good thing, too, seeing as how the three of them made a pretty conspicuous picture as they entered civilization again.

"Where to now, Herb?" Nicky Neill asked.

"That'll be the station yonder," he pointed. The red brick building was old but still proud. "I reckon we'll find a resting spot and lay low till it's time to make our move." He glanced around the area and smiled when his gaze settled upon a shed down track from the station. "That outbuilding ought to provide good shade, and cover too. No need to advertise our presence. The station master here doesn't take too kindly to hobos."

"Thank goodness we're stopping!" Ploox sighed. He paused to hoist a leg and inspect one of his boots. "I got a hole in muh right shoe. It ain't big yet, but it lets rocks in."

"Hang in there, Ploox," Herb encouraged him. "You just make do and we'll look into a new pair of slides in San Antone."

"Slides?" Ploox's brow wrinkled.

"Yeah," Herb replied, laughing. "Shoes, to you. I know of a spot downtown where a fella can pick up footwear real cheap."

"Well, okay," Ploox muttered. "If you say so, Herb."

They followed the tracks a bit further then left them behind, cutting across a field to the shed Herb had picked out. "How much of a wait you figure we've got, Herb?" Nicky Neill asked.

"Oh, judging by the sun I'd guess we can nap an hour or two. Why?" he grinned. "You got anything else to do?"

"No, I just don't want to miss the train."

"Hah!" This time Herb let loose with a real belly laugh. "I'd be more worried about Boxcar Fever if I was you."

"Boxcar Fever?" Ploox snapped upright. "Is that anything like chicken pox?"

"No, nothing like that, son. It isn't a regular sort of disease, but it is contagious. It's what happens to a fella when he hops his first shooting star and gets the feel of those steel wheels clicking away beneath him." Herb leaned back against the shed and sighed. "When a man gets all bedded down and gazes through that open boxcar door at God's great heaven, chock full of stars and the Milky Way ... then, by golly, that's when the fever strikes. You'll know all about it soon enough. I guarantee you, there isn't a doctor alive who can cure you once you're stricken."

They all shared a good laugh over Boxcar Fever, but soon afterwards things quieted down. Ploox and Herb lapsed into sleep, but Nicky Neill was too preoccupied with thoughts of his dad and Mexico to doze off. Plus, he had begun to worry about his mom and how upset she probably was. Herb was right; everyone makes choices. And Nicky Neill was discovering just how difficult some of them were to live with.

CHAPTER 18

"Whooo-ooo-whooo! Whooo-ooo-whooo!" A train whistle blasted in the distance.

"Herb!" Nicky Neill jumped to his feet and dashed around the corner of the shed. "Herb! Wake up! It's here! The train is here!" A steaming, snorting, jet-black locomotive appeared around the bend, sweeping over the same tracks the three of them had walked down earlier.

"Eh! What's that you say?" Herb mumbled, bounding upright. "Yeah! I hear it. She'll be pulling in soon." He reached down and gave Ploox a shake. "Cut the snooze, pal! Mr. O'Brien has arrived!"

"What do we do next?" Nicky Neill scooped up his pack and slid it over one shoulder.

"All right now, take it easy," Herb cautioned. "Here's the plan." He raised himself to one knee and peered around the corner of the shed. "We sit tight till she pulls into the station, see? Then we give her a little time to take on passengers and freight. Got to allow the depot to clear. That's when we make our move for those boxcars at the end." He pointed to a line of red and brown cars that made up the last half of the train. "Listen close!" he continued. "There will be a gentleman or two in the caboose. If anyone's going to spot us it'll be those fellas. So," he shrugged, "you still game?"

"Yessir!" Ploox squealed. Nicky Neill nodded.

"Good!" Herb hoisted his bundle over his shoulder. "Stay at the ready!"

They remained crouched behind the shed while the train steamed and hissed into the siding. Soon they could make out people's legs and the wheels of baggage wagons moving up and down the depot. But that was all they observed. Then the whistle let loose an unexpected burst of ear-splitting pressure and the locomotive began to chug forward.

"She's rolling!" Nicky Neill cried. "What now, Herb?"

"Durned their hides! They're sticking to schedule. We'll have to make a run for it. Come on!"

Herb sprang from cover. Ploox and Nicky Neill took off behind him. As they raced across the open field towards the slow-moving train Nicky Neill couldn't help but wonder how they would ever slip past the men guarding it.

"There!" Herb pointed to a rusty brown car in the middle of the line. "She's got a door ajar! That's our roost!"

Herb reached the car first and ran along beside it, pulling at the heavy door with one hand. How he managed not to trip over the ties was a mystery, but after the third or fourth tug the door slid back a few feet. He tossed his stick and bundle through the opening and then, with astonishing agility, leaped through the crack himself. Once inside he came to his feet in the doorway and beckoned the boys on. "Keep moving, lads! One of you, come alongside and give me your hand."

Herb wedged himself in the opening and extended an arm in the boys' direction. Nicky Neill was closest so he moved nearer to the lumbering train, as close as he dared anyway. Choices, he thought to himself, always choices. Then he was beside the car, dancing over the ends of the ties, staring at Herb's outstretched hand. "Now!" Herb shouted. "Now!" Nicky Neill reached out and slapped at Herb's palm. The hobo's hand wrapped around the boy's like a vise and with a mighty heave he lifted him off the ground and into the boxcar.

The train was clearing the station and picking up speed. Nicky Neill crowded close to Herb and peered through the doorway. Ploox was still beside them, running for all he was worth. His eyes were wide and a panicked expression covered his face.

"Throw me your bag, Ploox!" Herb yelled.

Without breaking stride Ploox slid his bag off his shoulder and hurled it at the opening. Herb batted it inside. The train was rolling briskly and Ploox was forced to sprint full speed just to stay even.

"Closer!" Herb pleaded. "Two steps closer and give me your hand."

Nicky Neill watched as Ploox bound onto the tracks, skipping over the butt-ends of the ties like a ballet dancer in some grotesque production. If he tripped, if he went down ... it was too awful to think about.

"Now!" Herb leaned as far away from the car as possible. In a final, gut-bursting fit of speed, Ploox flung himself at the opening, arms flailing. Herb lunged for him and caught an elbow. Nicky Neill latched onto Herb's coat and jammed both feet against the wall for leverage. "Urrr-uggghh!" Herb groaned and hoisted Ploox off the ground, swinging him into the car.

"I made it!" Ploox sang out, over and over. "I made it!" The three of them collapsed on the dusty wooden floor and cheered their victory. When the exhilaration wore off they crawled to the opening and stared at the countryside beyond. They'd done it. They had hopped a freight train and lived to tell it. They were on their way. A new feeling of confidence settled over the boys. From that moment forward Nicky Neill had no doubt whatsoever that they were invincible.

CHAPTER 19

"*D*idja ever notice," Ploox mused, "how the sun jus' kinda dribbles away at the end of a day? Like the whole sky's a big tub o' bathwater bein' sucked down some giant drain?" The trio was perched in the boxcar doorway, legs dangling, admiring the sunset.

"That's downright poetic, son!" Herb said, nodding in agreement. "Yes, sir," he slapped Ploox's shoulder, "downright poetic!"

In the distance scores of tiny lights dotted the countryside and every now and then a falling star would arc across the sky. Warm night air washed over their faces and, always, the rhythmic clickety-clack of iron wheels clamored beneath them.

"Whutta we do next, Herb?" Ploox inquired.

"Well," he yawned, "for now we just go with the flow and enjoy the evening. Maybe we'll have a bite to eat and then, when you're ready, catch a few winks. Our only concern tonight is switching trains in Dallas, and you can bet I know how that's done."

"Ya know whut?" Ploox eased back onto the floor and drew his backpack up beneath his head. "I like this way o' livin'. I think maybe when I grow up I jus' might git into this line o' work." Before long he fell silent and soon after he began to snore.

Herb and Nicky Neill talked into the night, mostly about Herb's life on the road. After a meal of sausage and cheese, Nicky Neill grew drowsy and slid back alongside Ploox. Herb remained perched in the doorway. Nicky Neill watched him until his eyes became too heavy to keep apart, but before he fell asleep he couldn't stop wondering how anyone could go through life without a home and a family.

When they reached Dallas, Herb woke the boys up and orchestrated their move to another train. The trick this time was to know which line of cars to choose. But Herb led them through the maze and installed them in another Johnny O'. Once aboard he informed them they would be in for a long wait, so Ploox and Nicky Neill simply went back to sleep.

Hours later they were awakened by a series of sharp, earthquake-like jolts. They were moving again. The last leg of their journey to San Antonio was underway. Like Herb, they had become masters of the art of come and go. Nicky Neill had no doubt that he and Ploox would be in Mexico within the next forty-eight hours. That night he dreamed of smashing pinatas and scurrying after candy.

CHAPTER 20

A thin shaft of sunlight pierced the boxcar doorway
and sliced across Nicky Neill's face. He awoke with a
start. It was early; Ploox and Herb were still dozing. Beneath
them the clatter of steel on steel persisted. Nicky Neill rolled to
all fours and shuffled towards the door.

The grasslands and wheat fields that he expected to see
had disappeared. Instead he looked out upon broad, rolling
hills littered with rocks and cactus and thick stands of bushy
little trees. Here and there oceans of blue and orange flowers
stretched across entire fields, appearing more like paintings
than real life. "Ploox!" he shouted. "Herb! Wake up! You've got
to see this."

They awoke, under protest, but crawled to the opening
and peered out.

"Wow!" Ploox exclaimed, rubbing the sleep from his eyes.
"We're in Texas now, ain't we!"

Herb sighed and sniffed the air as if he were inhaling a
bouquet of freshly picked flowers. "This is the hill country,
boys. Texas at its best."

"So what are we looking at?" Nicky Neill asked. "What
kind of flowers are those? And what sort of tree is that?" He
pointed to a long stretch of the low, bushy trees that grew
everywhere. Herb sidled up next to him and swung his legs
over the edge.

"New places, new faces! Eh, boys? Ain't that the way!" His
face beamed as he spoke. "Those scruffy trees are called
mesquite, good for cooking fires. And those flowers yonder
would be bluebonnets and Indian paintbrushes. Easy on the
eyes, aren't they?"

Ploox squirmed in between them. "They got rattlesnakes out there?" he asked, still yawning.

"Say," Herb twisted around to face them squarely, "you lads don't know much about these parts, do you?"

"No, sir," Nicky Neill admitted. "Not much. I do know the Alamo is in San Antonio though."

"That's right," Herb nodded, "and you'll have a first-hand look at it soon enough. We'll be pulling into town before long. No need for worry though. San Antone is a big city. You two will blend right in."

"How 'bout muh shoes, Herb?" Ploox lifted a boot within inches of his nose and poked an index finger through the dime-sized gap in the sole. "Ya say I can git me a new pair, cheap?"

"And what about a place to stay for the night?" Nicky Neill added. "We can't afford anything expensive, you know."

"Hmmn," Herb mulled it over. "There's a second-hand store not far from the freight yard. And I can recommend a good nickel flop, too, but there's liable to be a pack of those blasted bums hanging 'round. Of course, a cheap hotel ..."

"Whut's a nickel flop?" Ploox interrupted.

"Oh, sorry. A nickel flop is an all night movie house. Actually, it costs a quarter these days, but you get a warm place to sleep. And you can watch movies, too, if you like, although most of the flicks aren't worth staying awake for."

"Who cares!" Ploox smacked his lips. "Just so long as they sell hot buttered popcorn!"

"On second thought," Herb continued, "maybe that's not such a good idea. You two need a good night's rest. I think a cheap hotel would be a better idea. And I know just the place."

"Whoa! Hold on, Herb," Nicky Neill interrupted. "Why am I getting the feeling you won't be with us in San Antonio?"

Herb shifted his gaze beyond the door. "Listen, boys. You two have been the best of company ... best I've known in a long time. But I'm starting to feel responsible for you, see? I can't deal with that." He refused to look at them while he spoke.

"Anyway, finding your pop is your job. It's your adventure. I've got my own trail to follow. This train goes on down to Corpus Christi. I reckon I won't be jumping off with you."

At first, the boys didn't know what to say, so they just kept quiet.

"You two are born travelers, you're made of all the right stuff. There's not a doubt in my mind you won't find Nicky Neill's daddy. You don't need me anymore, believe me. I've shown you all I can. My chapter with you boys is closed." He raised his head to face them. "I'm just thankful we met and rode awhile as friends. When it's all said and done that's the best we have to hope for."

"Okay, Herb," Nicky Neill spoke up at last. "We understand. At least I think we do. What I don't get is why we're jumping off in San Antonio. Shouldn't we stay on board as long as the train is moving south?"

"Yeah," Ploox joined in. "Do ya jus' wanna git rid of us?"

"Oh, come on, lads! Don't talk like that. Surely you know me better?"

"Sorry," Ploox said. "But whut, then?"

"The reason you're getting off is because I have a friend there who can help you. He may be able to deliver you to Mexico."

"What?" Nicky Neill's enthusiasm returned. "Who is he? How do we find him? I knew you wouldn't let us down, Herb!"

"Look," he cautioned, "nothing's set in stone. This may or may not work out, but it's worth a try. My friend's name is Lobo. He brings people out of Mexico and finds them work in Texas. I don't see why he can't do it in reverse. Anyway, he owns a stall in the main market; it's called La Gran Fruta. Look him up first thing in the morning. Tell him we're traveling partners."

"You bet, Herb! And thanks for everything. I want you to know we don't hold it against you for moving on. Actually, I kind of thought this might happen." Nicky Neill hesitated, to weigh his words. "I, uh ... I guess you wouldn't be a hobo otherwise."

"So you do understand," he said. "That puts my mind at ease. Nothing worse than parting company under a dark cloud."

"Hey!" An important thought popped into Ploox's head. "So where we gonna stay the night? An' where do I trade muh boots in?"

"Ah, yes!" Herb's expression brightened. "The essentials! For a decent night's rest you'll want the Sueno Feliz hotel. That's Spanish for happy sleep, more or less. It's at the corner of Central and Rose. And the second-hand store is just two blocks west on Central. It's called Shorty's Thrift and Trade. You can't miss it. Everything else on that street is either a pawn shop or a beer joint." At this point his expression sobered. "You can see the sights of town during daylight, but come nightfall, stick close to your hotel. That part of the city can be nasty after dark."

"Thanks, Herb," Nicky Neill said. "We'll remember that."

CHAPTER 21

"*H*ey!" Ploox shouted out. "We're comin' inta a town!" In his excitement he leaned so far beyond the opening he almost tumbled off the ledge. Luckily, Herb was close by and managed to grab him by the collar. Nicky Neill crowded in behind the two of them.

"Yep," Herb confirmed, "Alamo City! And those would be the stockyards coming up." He pointed to a sprawling area of cattle pens and feed lots. "This is where you boys get off. Round up your gear and I'll let you know when it comes time to bail out."

As the train began slowing it lurched and jostled, but the boys managed to drag their packs into the opening and kneel beside them. By then, long rows of weathered fence paralleled the track and huge corrals sprang up at close intervals, most of them filled with wide-eyed, bawling cattle.

"Get ready," Herb signalled. Then he looked them over closely. "This isn't goodbye, you know. I prefer to say until we meet again."

"Sure. Okay, Herb," Nicky Neill nodded. "Until we meet again."

"Yeah," Ploox seconded. "Me too!"

They shook hands all around. Then Herb advised them to stand by. "Don't forget, the Sueno Feliz, on Central and Rose. And Shorty's Thrift further down Central. And see Lobo in the morning!"

"Got it," Nicky Neill said. "Lobo at La Gran Fruta."

"Yeah, that's right." Herb glanced beyond the doorway again. "Now! Time's up!" He slapped Nicky Neill's backpack. "Cross the tracks quickly, don't loiter! Then make straight for town." He hesitated a moment. "Jump! Jump you Gay Cats!"

Nicky Neill bailed out, with Ploox hot on his heels. They hit the ground and rolled a few times but came up running. As they sprinted away from the moving train Nicky Neill threw a hurried glance over his shoulder and saw Herb, still in the doorway, waving farewell.

The boys continued running as if someone were chasing them. Their dash carried them over a series of tracks before ending at a tall chain link fence. Nicky Neill hoisted a sagging section of wire and allowed his friend to wriggle under. Ploox returned the favor. They took one last look at the rail yard and the departing train before starting off for town. Herb was no longer in sight. As they began their hike Ploox sang out unexpectedly, "New places, new faces! Ain't that the way!"

CHAPTER 22

"*M*an-oh-man!" Ploox gawked at the irregular mountains of concrete and steel that loomed ahead of them. "This's a big city ... bigger'n Waterville by a mile!"

"No lie!" Nicky Neill was just as awed as Ploox, but he tried not to show it. "At least according to Herb, we're on the right side of town." He took a last look over his shoulder. "Come on, let's keep moving."

The boys headed straight for the heart of the skyline, winding their way through assorted dumps and junkyards and scurrying between sagging rows of abandoned buildings. At one point Ploox scaled a tower of used refrigerators and dubbed it Mount Cool. They laughed about it, but their laughter was uneasy. After Ploox came down from his mountain they picked up their pace and put the area behind them. A little while later they reached inhabited territory. The sight of other people was a relief.

"Well, okay then!" Nicky Neill turned to Ploox. "What do you want to do first? Check in at the hotel or see the Alamo?"

"Well," he hesitated, "ta tell yuh the truth, muh feet're killin' me. Yuh think maybe we could look fer that thrifty store Herb told us about?"

"You mean Shorty's Thrift and Trade?"

"Yeah! That's it. I need me some new slides." Ploox's face contorted into a silly grin. "I cain't be no Gay Cat if I got sore paws! Ha-ha-ha, eee-yuk!"

"Very funny, Ploox. Very funny." But Nicky Neill had to laugh. He'd never heard his friend make up a joke before. At that moment a man rounded a nearby corner and headed towards them on the sidewalk. Nicky Neill approached him. "Excuse me, sir. Could you tell me where Central is?"

"How should I know, kid?" he replied gruffly. The boys stepped aside and the man continued on his way.

"Friendly here, ain't they?" Ploox watched the stranger as he disappeared down the street.

"Don't worry about it. Next time we'll ask a kid."

The two kept moving. Before long they came upon a boy about their own age, perched on a curb, fishing for crawdads through a drainage grate.

"Hiya!" Nicky Neill called out. "Catching anything?"

"Naw, just killin' time."

"Could you tell us where Central is? Where it connects with Rose?" The boys waited for an answer while the kid pulled his baitless string through the bars.

"Yeah, I know where it is." He squinted up at the pair. "Go two blocks straight ahead from this corner, then turn right. That's Central. To hit Rose you have to walk another six or seven blocks." He shielded his eyes with his free hand. "But you guys oughta be careful down there. Ain't no kids in that part of town."

"Sure thing," Nicky Neill said. "Thanks for the help. See ya!" He turned to Ploox and grinned. "What are we waiting for, big guy? Let's get those slides!"

The kid gave good directions. In less than fifteen minutes they were standing beneath the sign for Shorty's Thrift and Trade. Nicky Neill politely took Ploox by the elbow and escorted him inside. A bell on the door jingled as they entered.

The interior of Shorty's took them by surprise. Clothes were piled everywhere, from floor to ceiling. And the air was thick, heavy with the scent of mothballs and old wool. A feeling of helplessness settled over Nicky Neill. The thought of trying to find anything specific was overwhelming.

"There ain't no place like this back home, huh?" Ploox was just as bewildered as his partner.

"That's for sure," Nicky Neill whispered. "But I've got a hunch that if you can find anything that fits it's going to be a real bargain."

"Think they sell boots?" Ploox whispered back.

"Guess we'll find out soon enough," Nicky Neill replied, resuming a normal tone. Just then a voice rang out across the aisle.

"Can I help y'all find somethin'?" Nicky Neill peered between two walls of dusty, cobweb-covered garments and saw a thin, gray-haired lady moving their way.

"Uh, yes ma'am," Ploox spoke up and walked forward to meet her. "I'm lookin' fer some boots."

"Well, young man, y'all will just have to follow me then."

As she turned towards the back of the store, Nicky Neill noticed a nametag pinned to her blouse with the name Lenore Stibley printed in neat black letters. They followed after her until they reached the shoe department. There must have been a thousand pair strewn along the floor or crammed upon makeshift racks.

"What's yore size, sonny boy? And what're y'all lookin' for, exactly?" Lenore Stibley's narrow, squinty gaze made Ploox uneasy.

"Uh ... oh ... lemme see! I take a twelve," he sputtered, "maybe a twelve 'n a half, I dunno. I want some boots, ma'am."

"My, my," she looked Ploox over. "That's a pretty fair size for a young'n yore age, ain't it? How old are ya, anyhow?"

"Thirteen," Ploox answered, blushing.

"Is that so? I declare. I got a grandson 'bout yore age, but he don't have no feet near that size." She turned away and began poking through a landslide of shoes and boots as if there were some sort of order involved. "All right! Here we are." She stopped her rummaging. "Ever'thang on these two shelves is yore size. Look 'em over an' take yer pick."

"Gee, thanks, ma'am." Ploox couldn't bear to make eye contact with her. Instead he scanned the mass of available candidates. Then his eyes came to rest on a pair of round-toed work boots. "I'll take these!" he announced, plucking them from the lot.

"Those?" Nicky Neill winced. "Why those?"

"'Cause I like 'em! They got style!" Ploox plopped himself down on a three-legged stool and let his pack slide from his shoulders. A rancid cabbage aroma immediately wafted up from his crusty socks and Mrs. Stibley stumbled backwards. Her hand flew up to stifle a gag.

"Hurry!" Nicky Neill pinched his nose as he spoke. "Get those boots on before we pass out!" Ploox giggled and pushed his feet into his prizes.

"Oh, man! Nicky-Neill, they fit perfect. Can I have 'em? Huh?"

"How much are they, Mrs. Stibley?" Nicky Neill asked.

"Them'll run y'all fifty cents." Her reply was swift. Nicky Neill fished into his watch pocket and retrieved a dollar bill.

"Here you go, ma'am." He offered her the money. "By the way, is there a restroom here?"

"Goodness, yes. It's in the corner yonder, behind the curtain. Be sure to flush, ya hear? I'll fetch yer change. S'cuse me now." She left the boys alone and disappeared between the stacks of clothing.

"Lace those boots up, Ploox. I'll be back in a jiffy."

When Nicky Neill returned, Mrs. Stibley was engaged in conversation with Ploox. Looking his way, she slapped her apron and began to apologize. "Land o' mercy, I got so caught up in talkin' to your friend here I done forgot I miscounted your change. I'll be right back. Don't go away!"

A panicked expression covered Ploox's face as he approached his friend. "Hey! That old lady wanted ta know whut we wuz doin' in the city with backpacks."

"Oh, yeah? What did you tell her?"

"I told her we wuz goin' campin'."

"Do you think she bought it?"

"I don't think so, Nicky Neill. I think she's up ta somethin'."

"All right, calm down. You stay put and I'll check up on her." Nicky Neill passed his backpack to Ploox and began to creep through the aisles in the direction Mrs. Stibley had taken. He found her next to the cash register, crouched over, whispering into the telephone. He dropped to his knees and moved closer.

"Yes, sir," she was saying. "Two young boys. An' they have money on 'em. Plenty I'd say." There was a pause. "Well, I know one of 'em is thirteen. What's that?" She paused once again as she listened. "Oh, yes, Sergeant! I'll do my best. I'll keep 'em here till you can send someone over." With a gasp Nicky Neill sprang up and hustled back to Ploox.

"She called the cops!" he hissed. "We've got to split!"

But Ploox was rooted to the spot. Instead of following after his friend he was staring down the aisle at Mrs. Stibley. She had moved in to block their retreat. Somehow she didn't look so old or frail anymore.

CHAPTER 23

*M*rs. Stibley had pushed her sleeves up and anchored her hands on her hips. She did not look like the sort of woman to back down from a confrontation. For a moment she stared into Nicky Neill's eyes. He knew from her gaze that she had them pegged. Turning them over to the cops was the grown-up thing to do — that or she saw a reward in it. Either way, she was determined to block their exit.

"The back door, Ploox! It's the only way out!" Nicky Neill remembered seeing a doorway on his trip to the bathroom. "Come on, man! Let's go!" But Ploox had turned into a statue, fixed in stone by Mrs. Stibley's glare.

Mrs. Stibley took several steps towards them before she stopped and wrenched an arm off a dust-covered mannequin. She meant business. If Ploox didn't act fast they were goners. A flash of desperation cropped into Nicky Neill's brain.

"Chicken fight!" he yelled at the top of his lungs.

"Whut! Where?" Ploox jerked his head around. The spell was broken.

"Grab your pack! And follow me!" Nicky Neill bolted past Ploox on his way to the curtain that covered the back hallway.

This time Ploox reacted. So, too, did Mrs. Stibley. She was not far behind, shouting as she ran, "Come back here! Y'all forgot yore change! Stop, I say!"

After busting through the curtain the boys sprinted the length of the hallway to the rear exit. But when Nicky Neill tugged on the rusty door handle it refused to budge. "Rats! It's stuck, Ploox! We're trapped!"

"Here, lemme try!"

Nicky Neill stepped back. Ploox wrapped both hands around the knob and began tugging and twisting for all he was worth. Just then Mrs. Stibley appeared in the corridor.

"Ah-hah! Gotcha now, ya little scallywags!" She hunkered down and raised the mannequin's arm above her head. Then like a big game hunter, she began closing in for the kill.

"Ooo-ooh!" Ploox moaned feebly and backed away from the handle, keeping his eyes on Mrs. Stibley all the while. Then he charged the door and slammed into it with his shoulder. With a loud "swoosh" it swung open and Ploox tumbled into a shadow-filled alley.

"Ploox! You did it! We were pulling the wrong way!" Nicky Neill rushed through the opening behind him, pausing long enough to catch the door and slam it shut again. "Get up, pal! Let's get out of here!"

Ploox raised himself against a dingy wall, attempting to clear his head. A fierce banging at the door, however, sent him scurrying down the alley, dragging his backpack at his heels. His partner was already ahead of him, sprinting towards the street at the end of the passageway.

When Nicky Neill reached the corner he had to hurdle a garbage can overturned by a pack of startled dogs. All kinds of trash littered the area. He started to shout a warning over his shoulder but it was too late. Ploox plowed into the debris at full speed and was cut down at the knees by the overturned can. Nicky Neill back-pedalled to lend him a hand. For an instant Ploox laid there, sprawled on his belly. His nose was buried in a mound of coffee grounds and other remnants of someone's breakfast. Before his friend could pull him up, he sprang to his feet and they raced around the corner. The wail of an approaching siren spurred their escape.

CHAPTER 24

"*N*ow whut?" Ploox sputtered through the garbage still clinging to his face.

"This way!" Nicky Neill pointed ahead of them. "We've got to find another alley." They were huddled at the edge of a run-down side street, not more than a half block from the thrift shop. The blare of the siren was closing in fast. "Come on, Ploox! Run!" They hustled down a crumbling sidewalk before another alleyway appeared. Like rats entering a maze, they darted into the shadowy tunnel and never looked back.

It was all the boys could do to stay on their feet, dodging and twisting down one junk-filled corridor after another. Hordes of sleeping bats exploded from their roosts as they ran past. When the scream of the siren finally faded away, they stopped to catch their breath.

"Over here, Ploox!" Nicky Neill gasped, struggling to talk and inhale at the same time. Ploox followed his partner behind a dilapidated garbage bin. There they slumped against a wall until their breathing was controllable. "Oh my gosh!" Nicky Neill sighed. "That was a close one."

"Holy cow!" Ploox exclaimed, clutching his chest. "I thought we wuz goners back there. Then, when we started runnin', I knew fer sure I wuz gonna lose yuh. Promise me you'll never leave me behind ... promise!"

"Hey, you know I'd never leave you. We're partners in this deal, and I mean right to the end. If you ever get in a jam, I'll be there with you, I promise."

"Yuh mean it?" Ploox sounded relieved. "An yuh know whut? I'll be there fer you, too. Honest."

"Okay, then." Nicky Neill threw an arm around his friend's shoulder. "That settles it. Nothing or nobody can break us up. But I do know one thing we have to fix."

"Yeah? Whut's that?"

"This is the last time I'm going to say it, I swear." Nicky Neill's arm slipped from Ploox's shoulder and he rose up to peer over the bin. "From here on we've got to be a whole lot smarter. Me especially."

"Whuddya mean?" Ploox came to his feet beside his partner.

"I mean I haven't been thinking like I should. For starters, that lady in the thrift shop heard me call you Ploox. Now the police will be checking their missing person files. They're bound to put two and two together and figure out who we are."

Ploox gasped. "Missin' persons? Zat mean our pictures are gonna be on the wall in the post office?"

"Not quite," Nicky Neill laughed. "But now that they know we're in town they're not going to stop looking until they find us."

"Oh, m'gosh! When the F.B.I. comes after yuh, yuh don't stand a chance! Maybe we oughta surrender?"

"Knock it off, Ploox! We're not public enemies yet. We're just a couple of kids. Anyway, I've got an idea. We need to make up new identities, new names we can use around strangers. So, what do you want to be called?"

A smile spread over Ploox's face. "Uh ... uh, lemme see. I know! How 'bout John Doe!"

"No way, Ploox! That's a police name. Try another one, something a little more original." Nicky Neill waited while Ploox did some deep thinking.

"I've got it. Jus' call me Alfalfa!"

"Alfalfa what?" Nicky Neill asked, biting his lip.

"Uh ... uh ... I know! Alfalfa Johnson."

"Well, okay, I guess that's all right. It's kind of unusual, but no more than Ploox."

"Who you gonna be, Nicky Neill?"

"Oh, I guess I'll go with Tom Twain, in honor of Tom Sawyer and Mark Twain."

"Wow! Neat-o!" Ploox was grinning from ear to ear.

"Okay then, it's settled. This is serious business. When we're around other people we call each other by our new names only. Got it?"

"Yeah, Tom! I got it."

"All right, Alfalfa. Let's figure out where we are and find us a place to stay for the night. In the morning we'll look up Lobo. Who knows? We could be on our way to Mexico by lunch time!"

CHAPTER 25

*T*he boys emerged from their hiding place and set off down the shadowy tunnel in search of daylight. Before long they reached a street. Nicky Neill instructed Ploox to hang back and keep an eye on their gear while he stepped out onto the sidewalk to look things over. The neighborhood around him was the pits. Broken glass and garbage littered the concrete and most of the buildings were deserted. Just then a patrol car swung into view. He ducked back into the alley and flattened himself against the wall. After the cruiser passed he set off down the sidewalk. As he neared the first corner he noticed a faded sign dangling above a doorway that read: COZY REST BOARDING HOUSE. Below that, in small letters, the sign said: Rent A Room For A Night, A Week, Or A Month. Reasonable Rates. Inquire Inside. He hurried back to his partner and found him right where he had left him.

"Whut'd yuh find?" Ploox asked.

"It's not the Sueno Feliz, but it'll have to do. The cops are still looking for us so we better get a move on." The boys gathered up their packs and hustled to the sidewalk. "No fuzz in sight," Nicky Neill whispered, giving the street another once over. "Let's go!"

"Hey!" Ploox shuffled along beside his partner. "Yuh think this place has a swimmin' pool?"

"I doubt it. But hey, we can't be real choosy right now. The cops are on the prowl and we've got to lay low."

"But I jus' wanna drink a sodie pop an' float around on muh back in some nice, cool water."

"Don't worry, Ploox, we're going to be doing some great swimming down in Mexico, I promise."

The boys walked on to the corner in silence, but as they made the turn Ploox spoke up again. "I ain't so good 'bout lyin' ta grownups, yuh know? You better do all the talkin'."

Before Nicky Neill could reassure his friend, an old man stumbled out of a doorway ahead of them. His clothes were grease-stained and tattered and he smelled to high heaven. With great effort, he managed to steady himself and wait for the boys to reach him.

"Heeey ... kiddies! Can ya spare a ... hic! ... dime for an old man?" He stuck a filthy palm in Ploox's direction and struggled to focus his gaze. Ploox stared back at him, wide-eyed. Nicky Neill took his friend by the arm and led him around the ragged figure.

"It's too bad for him, Ploox. But if you gave him any dough he'd just waste it on booze."

Tears began to form in Ploox's eyes. "Zat whut Herb called a wino?"

"Yeah. Pretty sad, huh?"

"But how does a guy git thatta way? Whut if he's some-body's grampa?"

Nicky Neill didn't answer him. Instead, he pointed to the sign that stretched above them over the sidewalk. "There she is. Let's go in."

When they reached the door to the Cozy Rest, Nicky Neill made one last sweep of the street. He was looking for police, but anyone else following them in this neighborhood was cause for concern. Satisfied they were in the clear, he led the way inside. A foul-smelling, rickety old staircase rose to meet them.

CHAPTER 26

*T*he boys climbed the stairway, pausing every few steps, expecting it to cave in at any moment. At the top of the flight they came face to face with an ornate wooden door. Nicky Neill pressed down on the handle and pushed. The door swung open and slammed against a wall. He stepped aside and allowed Ploox to enter first.

The lobby that greeted them was big and almost fancy, in a rundown sort of way. A thick layer of dust blanketed everything and the ceilings and walls were partially hidden by a continuous curtain of cobwebs. The only furnishing in the room that looked halfway modern was a pay telephone along the opposite wall.

"Lookit, Nicky Neill." Ploox pointed to a sign across the room. "It says there's a dining room here. We can eat right in our hotel!"

"Hmmn, we'll see about that. Let's check in first." It was then Nicky Neill directed his attention to the reception desk—a tall counter spanning the left side of the room. He was shocked to find a man standing behind it, studying them intensely. He couldn't believe they had failed to notice him. But he was there, waiting for them, immobile, like a spider anticipating its next meal. A shiver raced down Nicky Neill's spine. Against his better judgement he approached the counter.

The man on the other side was small and thin with dark, menacing eyes. His hair was neatly parted, plastered down with some sort of glistening oil. A beak-like nose protruded beneath his brow. A vision of a weasel sprouted in Nicky Neill's imagination.

"How do, boys?" he smiled, exposing a set of dull, yellow teeth. A limp moustache clung to his upper lip like a centipede at rest.

"Uh, fine, thank you, sir," Nicky Neill muttered. Silently, he cursed their luck. Compared to this guy a jail cell didn't seem all that bad. But it was too late to turn tail.

"So whut kin I do fer ye, gents?" The man spoke down to them in a slow, southern whine. "Are ye in need o' lodgin'? Or maybe yer lookin' fer the Boy Scout jamboree? Hee-hee-hee!"

The boys looked at each other and shuddered. Nicky Neill knew he was going to have to call on his very best acting abilities if he was going to pull this off.

"We'd like a room for the night, sir. If you have any left, that is?" Nicky Neill's voice cracked but he couldn't help it. At least his knees weren't knocking.

"Whatcha got in mind, kid?" The man's whine became a sneer.

"What do you mean, sir?"

"I mean we got all kinds o' rooms, understand? There's private ones and shared ones ... some got toilets, others don't."

Nicky Neill was confused. If a room didn't have a can where was a guy supposed to go? Out the window? Before he could clear the matter up the clerk continued his spiel.

"Then we got the honeymoon suites and basement bordellos. Take yer pick, buckos. Ever'thang's available."

"Well, uh, what's your cheapest room?" As Nicky Neill spoke he could feel his Adam's apple swelling in his throat.

"Oh! So it's money we're worried about, is it? Well, well." The man tweaked the ends of his moustache and continued to look them over. "I reckon the *Common* is the place fer you two." The way he emphasized that word made Nicky Neill cringe. He waited for him to spit, to rid his mouth of the taste.

"What, uh, exactly is the Common, Mr. ... uh ... uh ... Mr.?"

"Sleezak," he hissed. "J.W. Sleezak."

"Thank you," Nicky Neill apologized. "What is the Common, Mr. Sleezak? And how much is it for one night?"

"One question at a time, bucko!" Sleezak's gaze narrowed. His eyes became a pair of lifeless slits. "The Common's a shared room, like what I tol' ye 'bout earlier, if ye wuz listenin'! Or maybe you boys is the sort o' kids who don't pay no mind when adults're talkin', hey?"

The boys both wagged their heads in the negative. "No, sir!" Nicky Neill said. "We listen good."

"Okay, then. In the Common y'all share a room with ten beds ... most of 'em already taken. It'll run ye twenty-five cents a night. The washrooms is down the hall." He paused and glared at the boys. "Take it er leave it, don't make me no never mind."

"I guess we'll take it, for one night that is." Nicky Neill didn't know what else to do. The price was right and in the morning they would look up Lobo. If they couldn't get off to Mexico right away then they would find another place to bunk.

"Good, good! Glad to have such youthful guests in our humble home." As Sleezak took up a pen to enter the boys into his ledger a thought occurred to him. He laid the pen aside and began to rub his hands together. "Ye asked 'bout meals earlier, didn't ye?"

"Oh, no, I ..."

"Yeah!" Ploox cut his partner off. "I did. D'yuh serve real food here?"

"How much is it?" Nicky Neill added, shooting a glare at Ploox.

"Oh, yes! We must watch our pennies, mustn't we?" The meanness that had temporarily disappeared returned with a vengeance. "Whut's the matter, boys? Didn't y'all sell enough cookies this year? Hee-hee-hee!"

"It's the girls who sell the cookies, sir," Nicky Neill corrected him.

"Whutever!" Sleezak snarled. "The grub'll set y'all back another twenty cents each. Y'all want it er not?"

"We'll take it, sir. We can afford that."

"Good." Sleezak licked his lips. "Then it's settled. Gimme yer names an' I'll register the both o' ye."

"I'm Tom Twain," Nicky Neill said, without a blink, "and this is my friend, Alfalfa Johnson."

CHAPTER 27

S leezak entered their names in an enormous ledger on the countertop. When he was done he looked the entries over. "Farm boys, huh?" he muttered. Then, laying his pen aside, he posed a couple of chilling questions. "Whatcha doin' in the city with them backpacks? Y'all ain't runaways is ye? Ol' J.W. don't want no conflict with the law on yer account. No sirree, I wouldn't like that."

"Don't worry, Mr. Sleezak," Nicky Neill assured him, "my Uncle Rosco is meeting us at the Alamo tomorrow morning. We'll stay with him after that. We just wanted to see what it was like on our own for a day. Honest."

"Scouts honor?" Sleezak flashed a yellow grin.

"Scout's honor, sir."

"Hmmn, I guess that's good enough fer me. After all, it's a free country ain't it? You boys can go about however ye please. Just so's ye settle yer accounts."

"Yes, sir," Nicky Neill snapped, digging into his pocket. "Here's a dollar. I'll pay for everything now." Sleezak snatched the bill from the boy's fingers. Nicky Neill was surprised when he flipped a dime back at him. He expected him to claim that for his tip.

"All right, buckos," Sleezak moved from behind the counter, "follow me an' I'll show ye to yer room."

He led the boys down a short hallway to a strange iron contraption. It took a few seconds for Nicky Neill to recognize it.

"This here's the elevator, boys."

"Oh, wow!" Ploox was impressed. "I ain't never seen no elevator like this before."

"She's a classic," Sleezak hissed. "Built long before either o' you two wuz born. But she works like a charm and that's whut matters."

With the twist of a latch the heavy wire door swung open and the three of them stepped into the cage. Sleezak secured the door and pulled an enamel lever. Right away the compartment began to rise, creaking and swaying as it climbed the exposed cables. Two floors up a bell rang and they stopped cold. Sleezak depressed the lever and released the door.

"Goll-ee, Mr. Sleezak!" Ploox exclaimed. "This is the neatest elevator I ever did see!"

"Ye like 'er do ya, boy? Well, don't let me catch either one o' you two playin' on this here machine. Now go on, git out!" Ploox's smile faded as he cowered through the doorway. Nicky Neill followed after him, but he never fully turned his back on their host.

"Now, buckos," Sleezak thrust his head from the cage and pointed a crooked finger down the dim hallway, "yer room is the last one on the left. Number 13." Then he ducked back into the elevator and began his descent.

"Whew!" Nicky Neill sighed. "I'm glad he's gone." Ploox nodded in agreement. "Let's check our room, huh?"

"Wait a minute!" Ploox shuddered. "Did he say number 13?"

"Yeah, he did all right. But hey, good thing we're not superstitious! Right? In fact, for us thirteen is a lucky number. I mean, here we are, off the street. Safe at last. We've got a room and a place to eat. Tomorrow we'll look up Herb's friend in the market. I'll bet by tomorrow night we'll be in Mexico up to our ears in tacos and hot sauce!"

"Well, yeah," Ploox shrugged, "I guess yer right. It's jus' fer one night anyway. So, where's our room?"

The boys trudged down a dusty, worn hallway until they reached the end. On the left, just as Sleezak had said, was number 13. Nicky Neill twisted the knob and followed the door into the room. Ploox was right on his heels.

The room was shadowy and it took the boys a minute to get used to the dimness. Gradually, they perceived the place was long and narrow. A row of bunks stretched across the floor ending at the far wall. The only window hung ajar in its frame, opening onto an alley. A torn blue curtain dangled from a nail above the window, quivering in the faint, stale breeze. Nicky Neill walked towards the center of the room, groping about with both hands. Before long he made contact with a string. He yanked down and a bare light bulb flashed on from the ceiling.

"Swell!" Nicky Neill groaned. "It looks better in the dark."

"No kiddin'," Ploox agreed. "Hey! Where's the closets ... an' the dressers? An' how come there ain't nobody else's stuff layin' around? Yuh think we're the only ones here?"

"Not according to Sleezak, but maybe he's wrong. Anyway, I hope so. Come on, let's take the last two beds by the window. We can stash our packs under our bunks."

Just then, Sleezak's slippery drawl echoed over their shoulders. "Ever'thang all right, gents?"

"Yes, sir!" Nicky Neill answered, wondering how long Sleezak had been standing there.

"I come to see if y'all wuz hungry yet?"

"Oh, yeah!" Ploox perked right up. "I'm starvin'!"

"Well, then, come on down to the dinin' room. Nora's fixin' up one meal taday an' this's it." With that Sleezak spun around and left the boys alone again.

"Boy," Nicky Neill sighed, "that guy sure is creepy."

"Yeah, ain't he." Ploox agreed. "Hey, Nicky Neill! Yuh think we could git a T.V. in our room?"

"Come off it, Ploox! What do you expect for two bits?"

"Hmmn, I guess yer right. At least we git ta eat somethin'."

"Don't be too thankful yet. Let's wait and see what they feed us first."

CHAPTER 28

*A*s the boys stepped from the elevator and headed towards the dining room, Sleezak looked up from his desk and smiled contemptibly. "Eat up, buckos! This grub might hafta last ye a good long while. Hee-hee-hee!"

"Thank you, Mr. Sleezak," Nicky Neill responded. But as soon as he said it he wondered what he was thanking him for.

"Gee," Ploox mumbled, "I hope the food looks better'n our room."

"Yeah," was all the comment Nicky Neill could muster.

The old dining room was a scene beyond anticipation. It reeked of mildew and cigarette butts. The interior was crowded with broken down metal tables and dilapidated chairs. The boys made their way to the back of the room where they chose the least cluttered spot.

"Hey, Nicky Neill! Lookit!" Ploox pointed at two crusty geezers sitting against the far wall. "Look at 'em eat!"

"No thanks, I don't want to kill my appetite."

"But ya gotta!" Ploox continued to gawk. "I think they're drinkin' their food. Their mouths're practically in their plates! They're jus' shovellin' it in! My pop'd kill me if I tried that."

"Come on, man, quit eyeballing those guys. If they don't like your staring they might just come over here and box your ears."

"Whoa!" Ploox's jaw dropped. "Yuh mean they might slug me?"

"I mean they might rearrange your face and toss you out a window. We've got to be real careful here. In case you haven't noticed this place isn't the Ritz Hotel."

Ploox shifted his gaze to the floor, only to encounter a bigger shock. "Oh, m'gosh! Oh, m'gosh! Nicky Neill, am I goin' nuts or is the floor really movin'?" As he spoke he hoisted his legs into the air.

What had once been a beautiful hardwood floor was now splintered and decaying. And swarming over the rotting planks was an entire civilization of frantic, nasty-looking insects.

"Aaaagh!" Ploox cried out, gasping for breath. "It's alive! Lemme outta here!" He jumped to his feet and started towards the door, but at that very moment the king of all cockroaches chose him for a landing pad. Like some big, lumbering transport plane, the insect glided across the high-ceilinged room and skidded over the boy's nose, coming to rest on his elbow. Ploox sprang onto his chair and began to scream, but no sound came out of his mouth.

Nicky Neill watched in awe as the front of Ploox's jeans grew darker and darker. Then he snapped out of it and bolted off his chair to lend his partner a hand. He was just about to flick the monster off his friend's arm when a thick, greasy fist shot over Ploox's shoulder and nabbed the roach king right on his throne.

"Gotcha, ya filthy little varmint!"

The boys watched as the hand manipulated the oversized insect between a thumb and forefinger, squishing it to smithereens. Without wasting any time, it flung the carcass to the floor and came to rest on an ample hip.

"Howdy, fellas! The name's Nora. Now what can I do for y'all?"

The boys' attention shifted from that greasy, murderous hand to its very owner. Before them stood a massive woman dressed in a dingy gray uniform. A tattered apron clung to her bulging waist and a long, well-chewed pencil poked through an opening in her matted red hair. Huge droplets of sweat glistened at her temples and ran across her neck. In spite of her rugged appearance, her face reflected an honest smile and her voice had a nice ring to it. Ploox stepped down from his chair.

"Oh, hi," Nicky Neill stammered. "I mean, hello, ma'am. Thanks for saving my friend."

"Aw, nothin' to it. I been huntin' that devil two days now. So whut'll it be?" She drew the pencil from her hair and produced a wrinkled notepad from her apron pocket. "We got beans an' we got beans. Today they come refried with rice 'n' cornbread or ya can have 'em in soup along with cornbread an' a slice o' fried tomata. Take yer pick. Price's the same."

The boys looked at each other, then back at the waitress.

"Well, fellas?"

"Uh, gimme them beans ... I mean soup," Ploox blurted. "And d'yuh have sodie pop?"

"Oh, yeah." Nora jammed the butt of her pencil between her lips and began chewing on it. "We got warm Grapette and cold Alamo Cola."

"Lemme have one o' them Alamo Colas, please."

"An' you?" Nora turned to Nicky Neill.

"I'll have the refried beans, please ... and one of those colas."

"Gotcha! One bowl, one plate ... comin' at ya! Oh, by the way, them soft drinks is an extra dime each, not part o' the package. That okay?"

"Yes, ma'am," Nicky Neill replied, "that'll be fine thanks." Nora twirled nimbly on one heel and disappeared into the kitchen.

"Hey, Nicky Neill," Ploox leaned across the table, "yuh think if any o' them bugs fell in our food we'd be able to spot 'em?"

"Listen, Ploox, keep any more gross thoughts like that to yourself. If we're lucky this could be one of our last meals in the U.S.A. Let's just make the best of it."

"Okay," he agreed. "Sorry 'bout that. Hey! Here she comes." The boys watched their waitress weave her way through the maze of damaged furniture until she arrived at their table.

"Here ya go, boys! The house special! If ya need somethin' more just give a holler. Oh, that'll be twenty cents for the colas."

"Thanks, ma'am. Here's a quarter." Nicky Neill handed the coin to her, trying not to make contact with those roach-crushing fingers. "Keep the change, please."

"Why, thank ya kindly, fellas! We don't see many big tippers 'round these parts." Pleased, Nora headed back towards the kitchen, whistling a happy tune as she picked her way.

"Ugggh!" Ploox dropped his spoon and shrank back in disgust. "This soup tastes like dishwater!"

"Too bad," Nicky Neill laughed. "My beans taste like fresh airplane glue. At least the cornbread's half decent. And this Alamo Cola isn't too bad. What the heck, hold your nose and shovel it down."

"Man!" Ploox groaned. "I thought adventure wuz s'posed to be fun!"

CHAPTER 29

Nicky Neill had just forced down his last spoonful of gruel when he noticed a pained expression on his friend's face. "What's the matter? Are you choking?"

"No, it's just muh legs. I cain't keep muh feet up much longer."

"Your feet?" Nicky Neill peered around the edge of the table. Ploox's legs were quivering as he struggled to hold his boots above the floor.

"I'm afraid to set 'em down with all them bugs. Yuh think yuh could piggyback me outta here?"

"Knock it off, Ploox! Those bugs will scatter when you start walking. Besides, you better get used to cockroaches. They say Mexico has lots of them." Nicky Neill pushed himself away from the table. "Come on, let's go."

Outside, in the lobby, Sleezak was hunched over the pay telephone. "Yeah ... yeah ... yeah," he whined. "You'll owe me one." When he caught sight of the boys he slammed down the receiver and gave them a slimy grin. "Hi, boys. I wuz jus' thinkin' 'bout y'all. Hee-hee! How wuz lunch?"

"Fine, sir. Thanks. Very beany," Nicky Neill replied.

"So," he slinked back behind the counter, "what else can I do fer ye?"

"I was wondering, Mr. Sleezak, if I could borrow a pen from you? I need to copy some notes for my friend."

"But I don't need no ..." Ploox interrupted. Nicky Neill elbowed him to shut up.

"I'll just need it for a little while. Then I'll bring it right back, I promise."

"Oh, I s'pose that'd be all righty." He began to twist the ends of his moustache. "But don't lose it, kid, or yuh'll hafta pay up."

"No, sir," Nicky Neill answered as their host shoved an old

ballpoint across the counter. All the way back to the elevator the boys could feel Sleezak's gaze boring into their backs.

"Hey," Ploox muttered, as the elevator began its ascent, "why'd yuh gimme that elbow back there?"

"Because I'm going to write a letter home, that's why. And I didn't want that creep to know about it. Look, the less that guy knows about us the better. Understand?" Ploox nodded sheepishly.

After the elevator ride Nicky Neill went right to work penning a letter. Ploox plopped down on the bunk next to his partner's and started to fidget. After several anxious minutes he spoke up.

"Whut'll I do, Nicky Neill? I'm bored."

"Here." Nicky Neill reached into his backpack and took out a Spanish phrase book that he had borrowed from his dad's study. "While I tell our folks we're okay, you start studying. The more Spanish we know down there the better."

"But I hate readin'. Yuh know I ain't no good with books."

"Read!" Nicky Neill thrust the book into Ploox's hands. "This is a rescue mission. Times like this you have to learn to do stuff you don't normally do."

Nicky Neill settled back on the lumpy mattress and resumed writing. After a couple of false starts he finally finished a note he was satisfied with. It read:

Dear Mom, Phin, and Ellen,

I hope you guys are all right. I miss you all a lot. I know you're probably really worried, but you don't need to be. Ploox and I are fine. I had to do this Mom, because if I didn't you would have and I couldn't stand the thought of you alone in some jungle.

Please don't get mad at me for saying this, but if you went missing too then what would happen to us kids? Anyway, I'm really, really sorry I ran away but someone has to find Dad. Ploox and I are doing pretty good so far. This is only our second day and we're

already in San Antonio. Tomorrow we leave for Mexico, so we should find Dad in no time. I'll write again soon. I love you.
Your son,
    Nicky Neill

P.S. Ploox wants you to tell his parents that he's okay too. I talked him into this so nobody should blame him for anything. He's a good partner and we're both learning lots on this trip. We're going to be okay, I promise.

Nicky Neill folded the letter and set it on his pillow while he fished through his pack for the stamped envelope he had brought along.

"There." He licked and sealed the flap. "You sit tight while I run downstairs and mail this."

"Huh? Oh, yeah ... sure, go ahead." Ploox was so absorbed in his book he didn't even look up.

Nicky Neill left the room and headed down the dim hallway. At the last minute he decided to skip the elevator and take the stairs. When he bounded into the lobby he noticed Sleezak was not at his post, so he left his pen on the counter and headed out to the street. For once luck was with him. He found a mailbox less than two blocks from the hotel. With the note safely tucked away all they had to do was get through the night and hook up with Lobo in the morning.

CHAPTER 30

"Wow!" Ploox looked up in surprise as Nicky Neill entered the room. "That wuz fast!"

"You bet."

"So, whut's next?" Ploox grinned. "The Alamo?"

"I don't think so. All it takes is one cop doing his job and we're history." Nicky Neill moseyed over to his friend's bunk and sat down beside him. "Okay, big guy, tell me what you've learned so far."

"Well," he frowned, "this is hard stuff. I can barely read English yuh know? Still, it's kinda neat."

"Hmmn." Nicky Neill looked the book over. "Let's do a lesson together. Savvy?"

"Savvy?" Ploox repeated. "I didn't read 'bout that one here."

"It means do you understand ... at least, I think it does. Come on, we'll work together and see what we can learn."

For the rest of the afternoon the boys concentrated on the phrase book. By way of sheer repetition they managed to memorize almost thirty expressions, and that was after they learned to count to twenty.

"Golly, Nicky Neill! I always figured I wuz dumb. But now I know Spanish! An' it ain't even that hard."

"Hey, didn't I tell you? You can do anything you set your mind to."

"Yeah, I can do anything I set muh mind to."

"Say," Nicky Neill peered through the tattered curtain, "it's starting to get dark outside. How 'bout we hit the sack and get up really early? We'll have breakfast in the market and then we'll look up Herb's friend."

"Yeah, I am gittin' kinda sleepy. Say, I didn't bring no pajamas. Whut'll we sleep in?"

"You don't bring pajamas on an adventure! Come on, Ploox! We sleep in our clothes, just like cowboys do."

"Sure," he grinned, "I knew that. By the way, where's all them other guys Sleezak tol' us about?"

"You got me. Maybe they checked out and never told J.W., just to tee him off! Anyway, what do we care? If they do come in we'll be sawing logs." Nicky Neill eased back on to his bunk and tried to iron out a few of the lumps in his lifeless mattress. "You want to pull that light string, Ploox?"

"Oh, sure. G'night, Nicky Neill."

"Night, pal."

CHAPTER 31

*T*he boys fell asleep surprisingly fast considering that darkness had not settled over the city yet. In spite of the crummy conditions, Nicky Neill was having a spectacular dream when an awful racket erupted out in the hallway. Startled, his eyes flew open and his heart attempted to pound itself free of his chest.

"Camptown ladies sing this song, doo-dah, doo-dah! Camptown racetrack five miles long, all the doo-dah day ... hic! Hey! Whyzit zo dark in here? Hic!" Suddenly, a group of foul-smelling men barged into the room and continued to carry on at the top of their lungs.

"Lez haff a li'l light, Elroy! Huh? Hic!"

"No problem, Tater. I'll jus' give this string a little tug."

"Thass better," one of the men cheered as the bare bulb flashed on. "Hic! Now fer a li'l nap."

Ploox, who had somehow continued to sleep through the ruckus, sat up in his bunk and rubbed his eyes in disbelief. He was horrified by what he saw and promptly flopped onto his stomach, pulling the covers over his head.

Just then, two more ragged drunks stormed into the room and collided with the others. An argument followed with lots of shouting and cursing.

"Aw right! Aw right!" one of them bellowed. "Lez knock this off an' git zum shut-eye!" The one who had just spoken launched himself towards Ploox's bunk. As he approached his target he tripped over his own feet and initiated an ungainly swan dive, propelling him squarely onto the boy's back.

"Ooomph!" Ploox gasped as the wind escaped him.

Regaining his breath, Ploox pushed himself up with a mighty heave and the wino flew off his back, bouncing to the floor with a loud thud.

"Hey!" the guy groaned. "Since when duz mattresses fight back?" Rolling to his feet, the drunk stumbled up to Ploox's bed a second time and flopped down once again.

"Eeee! Git offa me!" Ploox began to struggle wildly and dumped his unwanted guest onto the floor a second time. Instead of ducking beneath the covers again, Ploox sprang from his bunk and scooped up his backpack.

"Nicky Neill!" he shouted. "Them guys're crazy. I'm gittin' outta here!" Pack in hand he leaped upon the nearest bed and carried out his escape, bouncing over the rest of the mattresses, stomping on every guy who wasn't able to roll out of his way. In less than five seconds he was out the door and gone. Awestruck, Nicky Neill remained motionless, listening to the echoes of his partner's footsteps as he flew down the hallway.

"Holy cow!" Nicky Neill cried. "He's really leaving!" In a flash, he pitched the soiled sheet away and groped about for his backpack. When he found it he jammed his feet into his sneakers and took off after his partner. "Wait up, Ploox!" he shouted. "Wait up! Wait up!"

At the stairwell Nicky Neill paused to listen. He could no longer hear his friend's feet resounding off the concrete. He did, however, detect the swoosh of the downstairs door swinging shut. He leaped into the inky stairwell, bounding over four and five steps at a time. When he reached the bottom he rushed into the lobby. There he discovered the unimaginable. The office lights were ablaze. Ploox was pinned against the counter wall, locked in the grasp of some big, Neanderthal-looking character, a burly hand cupped tightly over his mouth. Off to one side of them stood the willowy figure of their loathsome host, Mr. J.W. Sleezak.

"Leavin' a tad early, ain't ye boys!" he hissed. Then, smiling meanly, he said, "Too bad ... for you, that is!"

From out of nowhere, a muscled forearm shot in front of Nicky Neill's face and a rough hand clamped over his mouth. Before he could even attempt to escape another arm wrapped around his body, pinning his arms to his side. He knew, in that instant, what it felt like to fall prey to a python.

Part II

Escape From Armadillo Ranch Camp

CHAPTER 32

"**B**ring 'em inta the office, Harry," Sleezak snarled, motioning the men to follow after him.

The two gorillas dragged the boys alongside them as if they were a couple of rag dolls. Inside the grimy cubicle that served as headquarters for the Cozy Rest they watched their host fish several lengths of rope from a desk drawer. Right on cue the thugs whirled them about in order for Sleezak to bind their wrists behind them.

"Hey! Mr. Sleezak, are you out of your mind? This is kidnapping! This is a serious ..."

"Shut up, kid!" The man who restrained Nicky Neill slapped a beefy palm across his face. "Gimmee somethin' fer his yap, J.W. I ain't listenin' to this if'n I don't have to."

In short order the boys were securely gagged with filthy bandanas.

"Is there a back way outta here, Sleez?" The man who held Ploox spoke up.

"Yeah, yeah. This way." Sleezak bolted out the office door and led them towards the stairwell, pausing long enough to scoop up the boys' backpacks in the lobby. "Don't need no evidence like this layin' 'round, huh?" He smiled slyly to the others. Shouldering the bags, Sleezak pushed the door open a few inches and surveyed the darkened stairwell. Then, weasel-like, he darted through the opening and disappeared down the murky hole. The kidnappers followed after him, slinging the boys over their shoulders as they began their descent. With each uncertain step they cursed Sleezak and the inky tunnel he had abandoned them to.

Finally, at the bottom, Sleezak struck a match so he could see to unlock a rusting steel door. That accomplished, he poked his nose out and sniffed the air. Satisfied, he stepped through the doorframe. "All clear," he hissed. "Zat yer car over yonder?"

"Yeah, that's us," the big guy answered. "Listen, Sleez, I owe ya fer this one. I'll be back in the mornin' with yer cut, so don't git antsy, awright?"

"Sure, sure, Harry. I trust ya. After all, we wuz cellmates once upon a time."

"Right," he acknowledged. "Okay, Grady, let's load 'em up and blow this place. See ya, J.W." As they stepped into the alley, the men scanned the shadows before hustling across the pavement towards a battered '49 Mercury. Without wasting any time, they pitched their victims into the backseat, tossed their backpacks in on top of them and kicked the door shut. Almost casually, the two men clambered into the front.

"Okay!" Grady sang out. "Let's do it!"

Harry turned the key in the ignition and the engine sputtered to life. Slowly, they began to roll down the alleyway towards an intersection. At that point Harry switched on the headlights. Before they turned onto the street Grady twisted around and gave the boys the evil eye, followed by a piece of friendly advice. "We're movin' out now, boys. Don't do anything foolish, you hear? If you upset me I'll have to make it uncomfortable for you ... real uncomfortable." With that he pulled a toothpick from his mouth and snapped it in front of their faces. "Got that?" he snarled. The boys recoiled in fear, wagging their heads that they understood. "What's next, Harry?" He swivelled about to face the driver.

"I'll git us to a phone, somewheres. Then I'll make the call, jus' to let 'im know we got the goods an' we're on our way. Yore job is to keep an eye on them two." Harry poked a thumb over his shoulder in reference to the boys.

From that point on the boys cowered in the shadows of the backseat, listening as the two men talked about them as if they were a couple of head of livestock bound for market.

On and on they drove until Harry pulled the car over beside a seedy all-night diner. Without a word he got out and entered the greasy spoon. A moment later he reappeared and approached a pay telephone off to one side of the building. The boys watched him deposit his coins and dial a number. In less than a minute's time he was back in the car.

"It's on, Grady. Ever'thing's set. We meet The Man a coupla hours 'fore sunup. Hotdiggity! We got lucky tonight!"

After the phone call the two abductors began to relax. Harry steered the car back onto the road and Grady settled deeper into his seat. Soon they were cruising down open highway, slicing through a humid Texas night towards some terrifying rendevous. A new wave of panic swept over Nicky Neill. According to Harry, they would be meeting someone they referred to as "The Man." Anyone held in such regard by these two hoodlums had to occupy a higher rung on the ladder of evil. With all his heart Nicky Neill did not wish to move up that ladder with them. He did not want to meet "The Man"— and he could tell from the labored breathing beside him that Ploox felt the very same way.

CHAPTER 33

*T*he last leg of their miserable journey led them into lonely, rolling countryside. The roads were lousy, littered with rocks and bumps and bottomless potholes. The dust became so thick they couldn't see out the windows half the time. Finally, in the middle of nowhere, the old Mercury ground to a halt, perched on a low bluff, waiting.

Nicky Neill looked over at Ploox. He was sitting upright but his eyes were closed. It was obvious they had been kidnapped and were in the process of being delivered to someone. And it appeared that their mysterious journey was all about money. But why? Who in the world would want to buy a couple of kids their age? And for what purpose? What if, his mind began to scream, there was a mad scientist out there who needed them for some crazy experiment? Or what if some secret government agency was searching for human guinea pigs for a new type of nerve gas? Their only real hope, as long as they remained alive, was to escape. But at the moment that was not an option. Their wrists were tied behind their backs so tightly the circulation was all but cut off. No one but Houdini himself could get out of a jam like this one.

"Hey, Harry. You wanna smoke?" Grady broke the silence that had descended upon the car.

"Naw, I don't think so. I reckon I'll just sit here and keep an eye on the cargo."

Grady lit up a cigarette and flipped the still burning match out the window. "You're sure startin' to act strange, Harry. What's with you, anyhow? Back at the diner you were happy as a lark. Now you appear nervous as a cat in a kennel. You scared o' ol' Sweeney, or what?"

"Shuddup, Grady!"

"Hey, now, he's not about to hurt us. No sirree, Bob! We did him a favor, don't you see? He's been pesterin' us the last three months for more kids, ever since we handed over that sawed-off runt of a Mexican."

"I dunno, Grady." Harry ran his fingers through his hair and continued to fidget. "There's somethin' 'bout these two makes me nervous, know what I mean? They ain't yer run-o-the-mill street urchin. Somebody jus' might miss these boys an' come lookin' fer 'em." He paused to snatch the cigarette from Grady's hand. "You know whut the rap fer kidnappin' is? I'll tell ya what it is; it's life in the pen. I don't wanna pull no life term, no sir!"

Grady fished another cigarette from his shirt pocket and put a match to it. After a long draw he resumed their conversation.

"Relax, Harry! Nothin' rotten's gonna happen, I swear. Evrett Sweeney is too smart and too tough to get caught at this little game. He'll destroy the evidence before it ever gets that far. And he's not about to bring any pain on the likes o' us neither because we're providin' him with the fuel for his machine. Hell, he needs us." Grady's cigarette glowed in the darkness.

"Yeah, yeah. I know whut yer sayin'. I jus' hope yer right. I done seen enough prison walls ta last me a lifetime. I don't need no 'lectric chair neither ta top things off."

"Trust me." Grady thumped his partner's chest. "You'll have a wad o' greenbacks in your pocket inside of an hour. That'll cure all your woes."

Once again Nicky Neill was shocked by the raw nature of the men's discussion. They were hardened ex-cons. And their topic of conversation was just as cruel and desperate as they were. Life in prison! Electric chair! Whatever they were caught up in, it was serious business. Then Ploox began to murmur, "I didn't do nuthin' ... I didn't do nuthin'. Oh help me, help me, help me! Oh, Mama, help me, help me!"

Ploox's murmuring grew to a whisper, which expanded to a wail. Harry wrenched around in his seat and waved a tobacco-reeking finger inches from the boy's nose. "Knock it off, buster, 'fore I give ya somethin' real to cry about! "

Moments later, Grady sprang forward, craning his neck over the dash. "Car lights!" he announced. "There's a car comin' our way."

"Just so it ain't the fuzz," Harry mumbled.

"Aw, don't be such a worrywart. Come on!" Grady pushed open the door. "Let's get these kids outta the car and have 'em ready when Ev pulls in."

The men climbed out hurriedly. Harry reached for the door on Nicky Neill's side and flung it open. Without speaking, he groped about for their backpacks. Grady appeared at the door beside Ploox. "End o' the road, you two. Out!" But the boy didn't budge. "I said OUT!" Grady reached in and grabbed Ploox by the collar and yanked him clear of the backseat with a single jerk. At the same time a vise-like grip encircled Nicky Neill's neck and he, too, was pulled from the car.

Grady herded the boys over the edge of the bank of a dry streambed while Harry followed close behind toting their backpacks. In the middle of the wash they stopped. From that vantage point they watched and waited as approaching headlights bore down upon them.

CHAPTER 34

*I*n the wash the boys' captors crushed them together like canned sardines. They were a package deal, ready for delivery. Time became an inchworm, crawling along at a painful, slow motion pace. And all the while those headlights bore down upon them. Then, in a cloud of choking dust, they arrived. The driver killed the engine and cut off the head-lamps, but the parking lights remained on, peering out of the darkness like the eyes of some giant, otherworldly insect.

To the accompaniment of a harsh metallic shriek, the door on the driver's side swung open and the outline of a man loomed above the cab. The figure stepped around the door and began moving toward the boys. Sand and gravel crunched beneath heavy boots.

"Evenin', men," came a deep, rugged voice. The man behind the words towered above them all like a giant redwood tree.

The man they called Evrett Sweeney stood less than a yard away, scrutinizing the boys. He had an oil drum of a chest, tree trunks for arms, and in the orange candescence of the parking lights, a baldhead that glowed like a colossal wet onion. Then he stepped forward, stretching out a massive arm, and stuffed something into Grady's eager palm. "Not a word o' this to nobody, ya hear?"

"You betcha, Ev," Grady assured him. "Not a word. We don't want anybody knowin' about this any more'n you do."

"That's whut I like ta hear," the giant replied. "Now git some blindfolds on them boys an' hogtie their legs. I'll be leav-in' right away."

"Sure thing, Ev," Harry responded meekly. "Glad to help out any way we can." The kidnappers moved quickly, binding strips of cotton over the boys' eyes. Then they shoved them to the ground and bound their ankles.

"There you go, Ev," Grady sighed. "Them little monkeys won't be seein' no evil now!" But the big man didn't share in Grady's joke.

"Load 'em in the truck," he ordered. "An' their baggage, too."

The men snatched the boys out of the dirt and dumped them into the cab of the pickup. A few seconds passed and their bags came raining down on top of them. Then the door slammed shut and they returned to Evrett.

"Thanks fer the merchandise, boys. Don't bother callin' me again. I got all the hands I need fer now. If somethin' changes you'll be hearin' from me. Got that?"

"Whatever you say, Ev," Grady replied nervously. "Well, so long."

"Yeah, so long, Evrett," Harry joined in.

"Later," Evrett responded. With heavy footsteps he walked towards the truck, swung the door open and climbed in. "Git down, you two!" he ordered. With a swipe he knocked the boys to the floor. They cringed as the door slammed shut and the truck's engine roared to life. Then, with a stomp of the accelerator, the truck jolted backwards, swerved around and reversed direction. Another stomp and it lurched forward, laboring over the loose sand and gravel of the streambed. Through all of this Ploox and Nicky Neill bounced around like rag dolls, ricocheting between the seat and the cold metal of the floorboard. As they moved ahead Ploox's skull crashed against the heater box. After that he began to moan in wretched agony.

For the first and only time they heard Evrett Sweeney laugh. "Oh, hell!" he bellowed. "Git back up here an' make yerselves comf'terble ... unless ya like it down there? On second thought, ya ain't got no choice. If'n yer all bruised an' banged ya cain't work. So up ya come." A ham hock of a hand hoisted the boys onto the seat again. "Y'all got a little ride ahead o' ya an' a big day comin' up. So git some rest. Yore gonna need it."

CHAPTER 35

*P*loox and Nicky Neill settled back in a breathless, dreadful silence while their driver adjusted his massive frame to the shifting demands of the roadway. For what seemed like forever they stayed in the spongy riverbed, swaying and bouncing along as though they'd been abandoned on a cheap amusement park ride. Then they were climbing and the pickup's engine roared as if it might explode. Moments later they lurched into space only to crash down with their hearts in their throats. From that point on the going became much easier. They were on paved road again and that meant they were closer to civilization. With the first yellow light of dawn on the horizon, Evrett lit a cigarette and let loose a long, satisfied sigh.

Nicky Neill felt himself relaxing somewhat. They had been kidnapped by a motley trio of small time hoodlums and then transferred to King Kong of the underworld, but at least they were still breathing. Hold it! There was something else: neither Sleezak nor his two pals had bothered to search them, which meant they still had their money and all their possessions. If they could somehow manage to escape they wouldn't have to start from scratch. Nicky Neill shifted his concentration back to their journey and attempted to develop some shred of awareness for where they were and where they might be headed.

For what seemed like ages they rode along in a virtual vacuum. All at once Evrett lifted his foot away from the accelerator and they began to coast. Then he downshifted and they turned left off the highway and started down a rough gravel lane. After a series of twists and turns they passed through a forest and shuddered over a plank bridge. Nicky Neill toppled into Ploox as they negotiated a sharp right turn, then they crested a small hill and glided to a stop.

Evrett released a heavy sigh and pushed open his door. "This's it, boys, yer new home. Y'all better learn ta like it 'cause it's all ya got from now on. Sit tight while I fetch Berfel." He slammed the door behind him, leaving the boys there alone.

"Ploox!" Nicky Neill whispered. "You okay?"

"Yeah," his voice trembled. "Least, I think so. Where are we, Nicky Neill? Whut're they gonna do with us?"

"I haven't got a clue what their plans are, but I think we're still in the country. Listen, you hang in there. Sssh! Hear that?"

Not so far away Evrett's booming voice erupted in anger. "Slack, you lazy hunk o' buzzard bait! Git yore tail outta that bunk and hustle down ta the barn or I'll fill yer head with the kind o' dreams that leave permanent scars! Blazes, man! It's almost seven o'clock!"

He paused, and then he lit into someone else. "And you, Hensley! You best do a right quick rise an' shine yerself 'fore I yank this here belt off and strap my initials all over yore backside!"

Evrett's threats were followed by an awful racket as the two victims yelled and complained bitterly to one another. Then the sound of shattering glass filled the air, followed by the harsh clamor of metal banging against metal. A screen door slammed twice. Moments later a furious pounding of clumsy footsteps signalled someone's approach.

"Dagnabbit, Cleadus!" A voice erupted amidst the stampede, growling in a thick Texas drawl. "Didn't I tell yuh to set that infernal alarm?"

"Yeah, yeah, so whut? Cain't a man make an honest mistake 'round here? Whut's so all-fired disast'rous 'bout sleepin' in ever onc't in a while, huh? Now where in the blazes is they? Oh, ah see 'em, yonder ... hunkered down in the cab there."

The next thing the boys knew the passenger door swung open and several pairs of coarse hands hauled them from their seat.

"Whoo-eee! Looka here, Berfel, this 'uns a whopper! Ah do b'lieve we got us a real workhorse this go 'round."

While Ploox and Nicky Neill stood there trembling, Berfel knelt down and cut the ropes that bound their ankles. A surge of blood flooded into their feet and they moaned in relief. "Feels good, don't it? Well, things is gonna git better from here on out, yessir. Y'all boys is at the country club now. Haw-haw! Okay, jes' stand to fer a sec!" Berfel turned away to address his partner. "Cleadus! Git in the barn there and take a holt o' them dawgs. We cain't have our new hands all chewed up 'fore they even done a lick o' work, now can we?"

"Sakes no, Berfel. Them boys gotta work first so's to earn the privilege o' gittin' gnawed on! Ha-ha-ha!"

Cleadus produced a key ring and departed the area, jingling and jangling as he went. Soon the severe groaning of a heavy door could be heard swinging open on rusted hinges. The sound of the door was immediately drowned out by a thunderous clap of barking ... deep, rumbling, vicious barking.

"Ah got 'em!" Cleadus called out. "Y'all come on down now."

"You heard 'im. Git along!" With that, Berfel grabbed the boys from behind. His grip was fierce and his fingers dug deep into their shoulders. In that fashion he guided them ahead of him. "Here we come!" he bellowed. "Take a tight hold o' them mutts, yuh hear?" Then, addressing the boys again, he said, "Y'all best take a big step up now."

Ploox and Nicky Neill began to goose step in blind anticipation. They quickly encountered a tall obstruction, which they managed to step over. But there were no more obstacles. Instead, they were swallowed by darkness and the air became dank and cool.

"This here's the barn," Berfel informed them. "Go on, Clead, hit them lights now." Soon a series of clicking noises could be heard followed by a blast of brightness. The dogs ceased their snarling and fell quiet. "Open up number five, Cleadus. We can leave 'em with the others while we grab a bite ta eat. Hey! Speakin' o' chow ... whose turn is it ta slop the pickers, anyhow?"

"Yer turn, Berf, remember?"

As Berfel pushed the boys ahead the dogs resumed their menacing. They sounded so close Nicky Neill expected them to rip into him any second. Then their guide jerked them to a stop, cut the ropes at their wrists and shoved them forward. While Nicky Neill struggled to remove his blindfold a door slammed shut behind him, leaving a terrible metal echo in its wake. He had heard that echo before, in an old movie about Alcatraz. He ripped the bandana over his ears and spun around. The light was painfully bright, but between blinks he made out the image of a door. He was right. It was made of steel bars. They were locked in a cell, a prison cell. How would he ever get them out of this mess?

CHAPTER 36

"Where are we, Nicky Neill?" Ploox wailed behind his partner, still groping about in darkness.

"Hold on, pal. I'll give you a hand." Nicky Neill steadied his friend and peeled his blindfold away. Suddenly, every light in the place flicked off followed by a resounding crash as the heavy door at the entrance collided with its frame. In that brief moment of illumination the one sight the boys managed to glimpse was that of a pair of dogs—big, burly bruisers—racing towards their cell. They backed away in horror as the dogs smashed against the steel bars, snapping and growling insanely. They continued to threaten them for several minutes before they retreated into the shadows.

"Oooh!" Ploox began to moan. "Oooh! Mama, help me!"

"Ploox, Ploox. It's okay. They can't get us in here. We'll get out of this, I promise you. I swear, we'll get out."

Then, from out of the blackness, a young voice interrupted Nicky Neill's attempt at consolation.

"Hey, man! Don't be makin' no promises y'all cain't keep. 'Cause lemme tell ya, y'all ain't goin' nowhere. You hear me?"

"Huh?" Nicky Neill was shocked by the presence of another kid. "Who said that?"

"I did. Lawson Jones is muh name. I been two years in this here place, ever since they opened fer bizness. An' I'm tellin' ya now, ain't no escapin' from the Armadillo Ranch Camp." He paused a moment, but Nicky Neill kept still. "Yer new bosses," he continued, "ain't like nobody you ever know'd afore. These mens is the meanest, nastiest sons o' guns in the whole state o' Texas. Ever' one of 'em is done escaped from the pen, that ain't no lie. An' ol' Sweeney, he's prob'ly the baddest man in the whole danged world! That's a fact. Huh-uh, brudda, you boys is in a load o' hurt. You lissen to me now and save yerself a bucket o' tears: fo'git yo mamma and daddy 'cause y'all is lost souls from now on. Y'all best work at stayin' alive, one day at a time."

"Aw, shuddup, Lawson. Give 'em a break." The second voice came from right next-door. Nicky Neill groped his way closer, only to be stopped by a wall of solid stone. "I'm Jack Watson. Me and my brother Nate are your neighbors on this side. We been here over a year and it's bad, all right. But you guys'll make it. Just don't try anything stupid ... and don't go talking back to Hensley or Slack. And whatever you do, don't rile Sweeney the Meanie!"

Nicky Neill couldn't believe it. The barn was a prison filled with kids. He had to know more. "How many guys are in here, anyway? And what for? What do they do with us?"

"Amigo!" a Spanish voice called out. "My name eez Pepe Gonzalez. I been heer for three months. Before, we are tweenty boys, but now weeth you guys we are tweenty-two ... an' I am very sorry to tell you thees muchachos, but we are slaves heer. Thees hombres, they are very bad men. They make us to peek rocks een thee fields all day long. They torture us eef we don't do eet right ... eet ees malo, muy malo heer!"

"Slaves! What do you mean, slaves?"

"Just like Pepe said," came a somber reply from down the cellblock. "You'll see soon enough. Who are you guys, anyway? And where'd you come from?"

Nicky Neill strained to make out the other cells, but it was hard. The only light that made it into the barn came from nail holes in the roof and the cracks around the front door. "My name's Nicky Neill Carpenter and my friend's called Ploox. We're from Oklahoma."

"Oklahoma!" a startled voice cried out from the cell on their right. "Wow! You guys are really far from home. Listen, my name's Skeeter Wilson and you two're in for a rough day. You're gonna be pickin' rocks for ten hours in the hot sun and they'll be pushin' you extra hard just to see what you're made of. So get ready for it. Most important thing of all, don't cry! And whatever you do, don't try to run for it 'cause they'll sic the dogs on you and them Rotts'll tear you apart. I ain't lyin'. They'll bury you right on the spot if the dogs get you."

"Bury yuh!" Ploox gasped. "Oh, Nicky Neill. How'd I ever let yuh talk me inta leavin' home? We're goners fer sure ... we'll never git back alive now."

"Ploox, it's going to be okay, I swear. I don't care what any of these guys say, we're not going to rot here. My dad needs us way more than this place does." Nicky Neill made his way through the cool, black space within their cell hoping to comfort Ploox again. But as he groped around he bumped into something hard. "Ow! What's this?" He felt it over. "Ploox! It's a bed! There's a bed hanging from the wall!"

"Yeah," a new voice joined in, "and there's another one above it. You also got a ditty can under the bottom rack."

"Come on, Ploox, let's lay down for a while. If they're going to make us work all day we better get some shuteye. You want the top bunk?"

"Really?" His tone of voice brightened. "Uh, gee, thanks."

Once Ploox was tucked away Nicky Neill stepped on his bed and whispered into his ear. "Listen, I got you into this mess and I give you my word I'll get you out. Forget about what that Lawson kid told us, or any of the others. You and me are breaking out of here as soon as I learn how things work. For now, just remember this: you're the toughest chicken fighter of all time and that means you can handle this place. So don't be scared. We'll just do what they say and then, when the time's right, we'll bust free. You believe me?"

"Uh-huh. I believe yuh."

Ploox pushed his thumb into his mouth and was sound asleep in a matter of seconds. Nicky Neill slipped down to his own bunk and rolled over onto his back. He had to begin now. He had to start thinking and planning like never before ... or Ploox, him, and even his dad, were all doomed.

CHAPTER 37

*N*icky Neill hadn't been on his bunk for more than twenty minutes when the two dogs began to whine. Seconds later, a key echoed in the lock and the big door flew open. An ocean of bright sunshine surged through the break, flooding the gloomy interior. Straightaway the row of light bulbs that ran down the aisle snapped on and a cruel, surly voice violated the stillness. "Awright, ya greazy bunch o' field runts! Up'n at 'em! Rise 'n' shine! Slop time!"

Nicky Neill sprang from his bunk and moved to the cell door, peering through the cold bars towards the source of all the racket. He saw a rough-looking character haul a large metal container through the open doorway and load it upon a small cart. Then he returned to the opening and hoisted a bulging paper sack off the ground, depositing it beside the container. With a yawn he pushed the cart forward a few feet.

"Hey, Cleadus!" Berfel called out. "You gonna gimme a hand, or whut?"

"Yeah, yeah!" a voice responded beyond the barn. "Ah'm a comin'! Hold yer horses." Momentarily, a second man passed through the doorway. He disappeared into a room off the entryway and emerged with a large basket overflowing with pint-sized cartons of milk.

"Set yer milk down, Cleadus. We got the matter of a shake-down to carry out."

"Oh, yeah! Be right with ya." Cleadus exited the barn but quickly reappeared, toting a pair of backpacks over his shoulder. When he had joined his partner the two of them approached the boys' cell.

"Hide 'n' seek time, you two!" Berfel announced, emptying the contents of the packs in front of their cell door. "Let's see whut y'all brung us!" Like a pair of buzzards in overalls the two men picked through the gear. "Kid's stuff!" Berfel complained. "We don't need no more kid's stuff ... where's the money?" He looked Nicky Neill over for several seconds, and then set about cramming their belongings back into the bags.

"Look here, we know durned well yer mamas wouldn't turn y'all out with nothin' ta eat on. So cough it up 'fore I come in there an' pluck ya apart like a brace o' quail!" With that Berfel reached to his side and hauled out a heavy ring of keys. For several long seconds he and Nicky Neill stared at each other. The silence was chilling. Slowly, he raised the key ring to eye level and jangled the keys in the boy's face. Then he reached for the door and jammed a key into the lock.

"Sir!" Nicky Neill shouted as the bars swung open. "Honest! We're broke!"

"Uh-huh," Berfel nodded, stepping inside. "Git up agin' that wall."

"Here!" Cleadus ordered, stepping in beside his partner. He flung an armful of clothing onto the floor. "Git them city duds off and put on these here work clothes." Then, to his surprise, he noticed Ploox still sleeping in the top bunk. "Git that biggun outta bed 'fore Ah crack his skull!"

In a panic Nicky Neill jumped onto his bunk and began shaking his friend. But he was dead to the world. He may as well have been in a coma. "Ploox! Wake up! You've got to get out of bed ... now!" But it was no use. He was in hibernation. Nicky Neill was about to make another plea when Berfel shoved him aside and stepped onto the bed, rising to an ominous vantage point above Ploox's head.

"Hee-hee-hee!" he cackled. "A reg'lar Sleepin' Beauty, eh? Maybe a lil' spark o' lightnin'll bring 'im aroun'?"

Berfel's hand disappeared into a side pocket of his overalls. He slowly withdrew a long, silver tube and raised it above his head, waving it lazily over Ploox. "There's a' open invitation!" he grinned, pointing the metal wand at a patch of exposed skin between Ploox's T-shirt and blue jeans. "Rise 'n' shine, biggun!" A sinister smile spread across Berfel's face as he guided the rod to the bare spot. As the metal made contact he brought his thumb down upon a small red button on the handle and pressed against it. A sharp, crisp, crackling noise echoed near the ceiling.

"Eeeee-yow!!" Ploox shrieked and bolted upright so fast his teeth slammed together and his neck made a loud popping sound. "Mama! Mama! Mama! Whut's happenin'? Somethin' stung me!"

"Git yer feet on that floor, boy!" Berfel ordered, still smirking. "Now! An peel them clothes off."

Ploox bailed out with no further encouragement, but he looked to his partner for an explanation. "They want us in these uniforms!" Nicky Neill pointed to the pile of clothes at his feet. "They're serious about it!"

As quick as a wink they shucked their old outfits, but before Nicky Neill could slip into his new trousers Cleadus pointed to his feet and said, "Gimme them socks, kid!"

"Huh?" Nicky Neill hesitated. "Let me keep my own socks, mister. I ... I ... uh ... my grandmother made them for me." But Cleadus wasn't buying it. Instead, he charged across the cell and shoved Nicky Neill onto the lower bunk. When the boy's feet flew up from the floor Cleadus grabbed for the toes of his socks. With a violent jerk he tugged them off and watched as a green rain of one-dollar bills sailed out.

"Ah-hah, Berf! Lookee here ... pay dirt! Them's right fancy odor eaters, kid." Cleadus stooped to gather the crumpled cash off the stone floor. "Sonny boy," he said, his gaze narrowing, "if'n you hide one more speck o' anything from me, Ah swear, Ah'll turn ya inside out to keep ya honest ... an' Ah mean INSIDE out! Ya hear?"

While Nicky Neill finished dressing, Berfel and Cleadus tore through the rest of their clothes, hoping for another bonanza. But they were disappointed. Their dirty work done they stomped out of the cell, slamming the heavy steel door behind them. The boys were busy lacing up their shoes when

Cleadus reappeared and poked his face through the bars. "Lissen up, campers! When you boys is ready ta check outta here, don't fergit ta pick up yer stuff at the supply room yonder! We'll keep real careful watch of it meantime. Ha-ha-ha!"

Nicky Neill stared after Cleadus as he shuffled off to the room in the corner of the barn opposite their cell. Ploox, meanwhile, was studying his new uniform. "Hey, Nicky Neill! Lookit! These ain't such bad clothes."

For the first time Nicky Neill took a close look at the uniforms. Their T-shirts were dark red with a black emblem on the front. He grabbed the bottom of Ploox's wrinkled jersey and stretched it tight, clarifying the image. What he saw was a picture of an armadillo leaping over a rock wall. A bright yellow sun beamed down from above. Curved atop the picture, in thick black lettering, was the word ARMADILLO. Beneath the picture, in the same style of print, were the words RANCH CAMP.

"Armadillo Ranch Camp," he read aloud. "That must be why that jerk called us campers." Nicky Neill continued to study Ploox. They both wore the same style of blue jeans. Instead of a belt to hold them up, these pants had a thick band of elastic around the waist: one size fit all. Nicky Neill had a hunch these jeans were designed for work, the manual labor kind.

"Hey, Nicky Neill," Ploox drawled, "yuh reckon we'll be ridin' Shetland ponies an' lassoin' armadillos?" A goofy smile spread across his face.

"Yeah, Ploox ... sure thing. And in the evenings we'll all sit around a big campfire and roast weenies with our counselors."

"Really!" he beamed. "Do yuh really think..."

At that moment Cleadus wheeled his little cart alongside their cell door and stopped. "Here ya go, hombres! The camp special. We like ta call it breakfast barf. Git it? Barf! Ha-ha-ha! Oooo-eee! Ah shore 'nuff got me a way with words, don't Ah, Berfy?"

Still laughing, Cleadus pulled two metal trays out of a drawer and set them on a narrow shelf affixed to the cart. Then he lifted the lid off the container, reached inside and drew out a ladle overflowing with thick green goop. Clumsily, he plopped two scoops of the unidentifiable ooze onto each tray. Replacing the ladle, he dipped a grimy paw into the paper sack beside the container and withdrew several large chunks of bread, which he deposited atop the shimmering green mounds. The ritual completed, he slid the trays beneath the cell door.

"Eat 'em up, boys! Eat 'em up! It wuz hot an hour ago, but ye'll jus' hafta make do now." He pressed his face up close against the bars and whispered, "An ya best chow down right proper, guys, 'cause yer gonna need ever' ounce o' energy yer scrawny li'l bodies got. Git muh drift?" Then, as an afterthought, he said, "Oh! Ah almost fergot. Drink this cow whiz." He thrust his hand towards the basket and pulled out several small cartons of milk. In a gesture of obvious disgust, he crammed four cartons through the bars and dropped them to the floor. "Growin' boys, right?"

But Nicky Neill hardly heard his comment. He was too hypnotized by his first real close-up of Cleadus's face, and the sight of him leering through the bars was an unforgettable experience. Salt and pepper whisker stubble crowded his face like a dirty shadow, but it didn't hide the long, jagged red scar that ran from the corner of his left eye to his chin. And just where the scar ended a huge brown mole took over, with long, wiry hairs poking out of it. When his mouth cracked open into that creepy grin a crooked row of stained teeth peered out, highlighted by several dark gaps in between where teeth used to be. The most unusual aspect of his face, however, were his eyes. The left eye was such a light blue that it almost appeared white, while the right one was deep blue with a nearly invisible pupil. Poking out between those strange eyes was an irregular beak of a nose.

"Ho-leee-cow!" Nicky Neill whispered after Cleadus had moved on to the next cell. "Did you see that face?"

"Uh-huh," Ploox muttered, backing away from the door. "I seen it all right, an' I seen it before, too."

"Where? Where have you ever seen that kisser before?"

"In nightmares!" he swallowed. "That's where."

CHAPTER 38

"Come on, Ploox, let's eat. I doubt if this is a three course breakfast."

The boys sat down on the edge of Nicky Neill's bunk and balanced their trays on their laps. Nicky Neill watched as Ploox slid his spoon into the heart of that quivering green substance and hoisted a full load to his waiting mouth. An expression of horror instantly flooded his face. Then he began to cough and spit, spewing green slime onto the opposite wall. "Ughhh! Argggh!" he gagged. "This stuff's poison! I swallowed poison!"

"Come on, Ploox, it can't be that bad. Look." Nicky Neill wrapped his lips around a small spoonful and smiled at his partner. Only his smile was short lived. As soon as his taste buds encountered the mucous ooze he launched into a coughing spasm of his own. Once he managed to catch his breath he nodded meekly to his friend. "Oooh, golly! You were right. It is that bad!"

They decided to let the main course rest in peace and concentrate on the bread and milk. But all too soon it was gone.

"Hey, Nicky Neill!" Ploox pricked an ear toward the cellblock. "Listen! Whut's that noise?"

An awful clanging and clattering had erupted in the direction of the entrance. It sounded like someone was lugging a load of chain across a stone floor. The boys set their trays on the bunk and eased towards the cell door for a look.

"Cell eleven, fall out! An' don't fergit them trays." Berfel stood silhouetted against the open doorway. Over his shoulders he carried a swarm of long chains. They dragged limp and lifeless behind him like dead snakes. Cleadus, too, toted a bunch of the same stuff, but his main duty was to unlock the cell doors and restrain the murderous pair of dogs. Ploox and Nicky Neill continued to watch as the scene unfolded.

The process went this way: two boys would emerge from their cell, food trays in hand. While Cleadus held the mutts at bay, Berfel knelt beside the prisoners and attached a shackle to each of their ankles. That done, the boys remained motionless and the two men moved on to the next cell. Paying strict attention, Nicky Neill noticed a few minor details. For one thing, a single length of chain bound cellmates together. Item two: both Cleadus and Berfel sported lethal-looking shotguns, slung across their shoulders amidst the chains. Item three: as the dogs moved from cell to cell their state of agitation increased. By the time the crew arrived at the boys' door those canines had worked themselves into a real dither. Thick, glistening streams of foam and saliva dangled from their snapping jaws and the chorus of snarling intimidation was practically deafening. The message radiating from their bulging eyes was straightforward: murder, pure and simple.

"Okay, you two!" Cleadus bellowed over the din. "Clear out!" While he waited for them to step forward he rolled his tongue inside his cheek and let fly with a whopping spurt of tobacco juice. "Splat!" It struck the back of the cell and the coffee-colored spittle began to meander down the wall. "Hey! You miserable li'l snot pumps!" he shouted again. "Clear out! Now!"

With a single giant step Ploox sprang from the cell and snapped to attention in front of Berfel. "Chunk!" went the manacle as it closed around his ankle. Nicky Neill was next. "Chunk!" The sound repeated itself and the boys became an inseparable team. Five minutes later the procedure was done. Every pair of prisoners in the barn had been secured.

"Awright, chainmates!" Cleadus screamed. "Hit it!" Automatically, the boys across the aisle from Ploox and Nicky Neill faced to their right. The boys on their side of the barn spun left. Then they began to march in single file towards the door. As each prisoner approached the exit he paused to empty the contents of his tray into a bucket. After that the tray itself was dumped into a tub of murky water and the prisoner stepped through the opening into daylight.

"What's next?" Nicky Neill whispered to one of the Watson brothers.

"Sssh! Don't talk, or you'll get the lightnin' rod. Next we board the truck. Just do like everyone else."

As Nicky Neill stepped clear of the barn a rumbling noise signalled the arrival of a big flatbed truck. Wooden sides had been added to the truck bed and two long rows of benches had been built into the walls. A dusty canvas canopy stretched over the top.

"Load 'em up!" Berfel commanded. As he spoke he pulled down a short ladder connected to the truck's frame. Like well-trained soldiers the prisoners mounted the ladder, holding the slack in their chain up to keep from tripping over it. Once on board they marched to the front of the bed and plopped down on the benches, eyes fixed ahead of them, mouths closed tight. Ploox and Nicky Neill clambered aboard like everyone else and took their places. As they settled in, Nicky Neill noticed most of the guys were trying to catch a glimpse of them while they pretended to stare straight ahead.

"Hey, new kid!" Berfel screamed. "Eyes front! Hear me? Ya don't see nothin'!"

When everyone was on board, Berfel slid the ladder back into place and waved a signal to someone waiting beyond the barn. Not long after, the old Dodge pickup rolled into view, navigated by none other than Evrett himself ... otherwise known as Sweeney the Meanie. Nicky Neill decided to risk it and swivelled his head around for a better view. He was startled to find another pair of Rottweiler dogs secured to the back of the truck. While the Dodge idled behind them, Cleadus commanded his pets to jump aboard and join the others. Once on, he snapped their leashes to an iron ring and joined Evrett in the cab. Berfel, meanwhile, had climbed behind the wheel of the boys' truck and was busily revving the engine and adjusting the mirror on his door. With a honk from the pickup they started to roll.

CHAPTER 39

As the big truck chugged forward Nicky Neill attempted to gain a clearer picture of their surroundings. The barn was the most obvious feature. It was huge, built entirely of fieldstone, except for the roof, which was weathered tin. From the looks of it, a direct hit from a nuclear bomb was the only thing that might shake it. It wasn't situated out in the open either, but rather in a natural bowl. Big hills rose up behind it on the east. To the west the land sloped sharply, disappearing into a line of trees. Before Nicky Neill could look any further the truck began to pick up speed. Right away a thick, choking blanket of dust billowed over the tail of the rig, swirling into everyone's noses and eyes. Sweeney's pickup began to drop back, trailing them at a more comfortable distance. That interval gave them their first real taste of freedom all morning. Before they had recovered from soil inhalation the boys were bombarded with questions.

"How'd they git ya?" someone shouted out.

"Who won the World Series last year?"

"Where'd they catch y'all? Did y'all run away from home?"

"What did you say your names were?"

"Wait a minute! Hold it!" Things quieted down. "There. That's better. I'm Nicky Neill and this is my friend, Ploox. We were on our way to Mexico, but we got kidnapped in San Antonio. We ran away from home three days ago to find my dad. He's lost in the jungle. Oh, and the Braves won the Series last year. Now, someone tell us, where are we? What's going on? And who are these weird guys bossing us around, anyway?"

A small, sincere-looking Mexican kid across the aisle tapped Nicky Neill on the knee. "Amigo, I am Pepe Gonzalez. Like I tell you before, we are slaves heer. Thees shirt, eet say

Armadillo Ranch Camp, but we are not campers. Ha! We are slaves. All day we peek rocks so thee boss mens can sell theem for beeg money een thee city. Eef we try to eescape they shoot us, or thee dogs geet you."

"Pepe!" Nicky Neill shouted over the rumbling of the tires. "How many guys have tried to escape?"

Pepe, and everyone around him, stared back at him in disbelief. A kid down the bench shook his head. "Listen!" he yelled. "No one escapes. There's been two tries and that's it. That means four guys went down ... permanent! You work here, or you die. But you never get away."

"Why duh they do this?" Ploox's foghorn voice boomed out loud and clear. "An' who owns this joint?"

A thin black kid at the front of the truck waved his hand. Everyone stopped their muttering and listened up. He began speaking effortlessly over the noise of the motor and the grumbling tires. "There's a millionaire owns this place, name o' Snodgrass. Way I figger, he musta had a lousy chil'hood. He's the one who busted Sweeney an' them other two clowns outta prison, so's they could do his dirty work for him. That's all we know 'bout Snotty, 'cept, o' course, he gits his satisfaction in life seein' us kids suffer. An' them cons," he continued, "for their part they gits to be bossmen an' make theirselves a pile o' dough. And that, my friend," he looked Nicky Neill square in the eye, "is the whole story."

"What's your name?" Nicky Neill asked.

"Alvin Dodd," he answered. "Outta Houston." He smiled like a kindly old man would smile.

About that time Lawson Jones leaned forward and eyeballed the boys. After giving them a good looking over he shouted, "Where'd they run across y'all boys, anyway? A Sunday school picnic?"

Nicky Neill could feel his face turning red while the rest of the crew had a good laugh on him and Ploox. "No, I told you. They kidnapped us in San Antonio, in an old hotel."

Lawson stared meanly. "I's fum Houston muhself an' I reckon I could whup the two o' y'all with one han' tied behind muh back. Whatcha think 'bout that, kid?"

Rather than make a bad situation worse Nicky Neill decided to bite his lip and sit tight. But Lawson wouldn't let it go.

"You thinks you tough, kid, don'tcha? Well, lemme tell y'all somethin'. I been pickin' rocks fer Sweeney an' them other baboons goin' on two years now. I'm tougher 'n a cast iron skillet, an' I knows damn well I could whup a world a hurt on a couple o' marshmellas like y'all. I seen other wimps like you boys come 'n' go in this place ... an' I kin tell jus' fum lookin' at ya that y'all won't last long. Um-uh, no sirree!"

Nicky Neill stared at him in reply. Ploox kept his eyes riveted to the floor.

"Hey!" he continued. "Whut podunk place you say y'all wuz fum? Shoot, you ain't nuthin' but a couple o' hicks fum the sticks! And yore friend there," he pointed to Ploox, "he's 'bout the dumbest lookin' kid I ever did see!" He was staring at Ploox now, who had become instantly pertified. "Hey, kid!" he shouted. "Why don'tcha wipe that nose? All that green stuff dribblin' 'crosst yer face is makin' me sick."

Nicky Neill didn't mind taking Lawson's razz himself, but he couldn't stand it when anyone made fun of Ploox the way he was. "Leave him alone, kid."

"Oh," Lawson smiled, "we talks back, do we? I'll show ya a thing er two later, boy."

That did it.

"Why don't you show me now, big mouth!" Nicky Neill lunged for him with outstretched arms. But before they could reach each other the guys around them caught them and pulled them back to the bench.

"Knock it off, Lawson," said a kid who was struggling to hold him. "We got enough trouble without you picking on every new kid who comes in here."

Everyone on the truck settled down after that. Nicky Neill used the peace to check out the rest of the group. On the bench across from him sat ten boys. On his bench there were twelve more, including Ploox and himself.

He shifted his attention to the countryside. Through the veil of dust he could make out gently rolling hills sparsely covered with squatty vegetation and tight clumps of mesquite trees. Here and there patches of low forest bordered the occasional ravine. Dry creek beds meandered aimlessly across the landscape. And everywhere there were rocks, scattered over the parched earth like crumbs beneath a kitchen table.

Without warning, the kid next to him jabbed his elbow into Nicky Neill's ribs. "Get ready! We're fixin' to stop."

Nicky Neill looked to the sky. The morning sun was in full blaze and there wasn't a cloud in sight. High overhead a vulture circled. He seemed to be watching them. Waiting.

CHAPTER 40

*T*heir driver knew only one way to use his brakes. He either left the pedal alone or he stomped it; there was no in between. At this moment he was stomping. There was a rude, high-pitched squeal as the brakes locked, followed by a tremendous shudder beneath the bed. The next thing the boys knew, they had all been launched off their benches. Ploox and Nicky Neill were catapulted onto the backs of their neighbors and then slammed back down against the railing.

They all sat quietly, choking in the dust cloud that followed after them, while the trailing pickup eased alongside. Cleadus killed the engine and hopped down from the cab. As he ambled to the rear of the truck the four dogs broke into their patented frenzy of snarling and barking, baring their yellowed fangs and straining against their leashes.

"Okie-dokie, boys!" Berfel crowed, sliding from the pickup. "Time we wuz gittin' some work in!" He stomped around to the end of the bed and pulled the ladder down, ordering everyone to file off. As the boys climbed down Cleadus observed them suspiciously. He had already retrieved his pair of mutts. They lunged repeatedly, twisting him first to one side and then the other. His shotgun was at the ready too and there was a real risk all the jerking and pulling by the dogs might cause it to go off.

"Two lines!" Cleadus screamed. "Keep to yer cell block!" Without saying a word, the boys followed his command. When everyone was assembled, Berfel turned away and collected his own dogs from the pickup bed.

"Awright, you crum bums!" he bellowed, returning to his position opposite Cleadus. "My crew, move out!" With a surprisingly nimble move he jumped ahead and led the way, marching toward a low shade tree that stood like a solitary island in the middle of a motionless sunbaked ocean.

The distance to the tree appeared to be about two hundred yards. With every step the chain rattled along between Ploox and Nicky Neill, joining the chorus of chains, adding to a rhythm that was both haunting and painful.

Right away, Ploox and Nicky Neill had problems. Even though the slender chain didn't look it, it was heavy and its weight caused the ankle clasps to bite into their flesh. Furthermore, with every root or rock the chain dragged across it would snag and jerk back on them viciously. After a few minutes two hundred yards began to look more like two miles.

"Pssst! Hey, Nicky Neill!" hissed one of the guys behind them. "Pick your chain up ... both of ya. It's easier and it don't hurt ya so bad thataway."

Without breaking stride, the boys scooped up a section of chain, eliminating the slack between them. The going became easy again. Nicky Neill twisted his head around to see who had done them the favor. "What's your name?" he asked.

"Bobby Burkett." In spite of the circumstances he smiled broadly. "My partner's name is Dwight Schlinkman, but just call him Schlink. Everyone else does. We're from San Antonio. Welcome to Armadillo Ranch Camp."

When they neared the tree they stopped, all of them but Berfel that is. He continued into the shade and then turned to face them, legs spread, hands on his hips. The killer dogs were fastened to a ring on his belt. His shotgun dangled casually from his shoulder. At his side, bobbing and swaying with each lunge of the hounds, hung one of those lightning rods. A weird thought flashed through Nicky Neill's head, suggesting that he and Ploox had actually died in the wreck with Leon and had been banished to some miserable outpost in hell. Was this his punishment for running away from home?

"Whoa! Hold it right there, you donkeys!" Berfel held up a hand, ordering them to stay put. "Y'all won't feel this shade tree 'til break time. Meanwhile, we got us a couple o' new boys this mornin', and y'all know whut that means, don'cha?"

Nicky Neill looked around to see the rest of the prisoners bobbing their heads in acknowledgment. Berfel went on with his lecture.

"It means," he grinned cruelly, "the rest o' ya get a li'l break right off the bat so's we can see whut sort o' pickers these newbies is." The grin faded from his unshaven face. "'Cause there's one thang we cain't stand on this here job, right? We cain't tolerate no slackers! That'd mean the rest o' the crew would hafta work harder ta make up fer them's that's not carryin' their load. Kinda like ol' Gonzalez there!" He cast a greasy eye in the undersized boy's direction.

Pepe lowered his head to escape the attention.

"Yep, boys," Berfel continued, shifting his gaze to Ploox and Nicky Neill, "Mr. Gonzalez is whut Ah call a Mex'can jumpless bean. He don't work hard 'nuff, so the rest o' the gang ends up havin' ta stay out here longer jus' to make up fer his shortcomin'. Now don't git me wrong, fellas. It don't make me no nevermind if'n you squirts hafta do overtime in this heat, 'cause eckercise builds strong bodies! Right?" It was becoming clear that Slack enjoyed the sound of his own voice. "Ha-ha! Nope!" He did a little crow hop for emphasis. "The catch is, me an' Cleadus gotta stay out here with y'all ... an' we hate overtime! Git muh drift?"

There was nothing for Ploox and Nicky Neill to do but nod in agreement. They had no idea what he was talking about, really. But they knew they were in for a learning experience.

CHAPTER 41

*B*erfel strode from beneath the boughs of the shade tree, making straight for Ploox and Nicky Neill. The boys weren't worried so much about him as they were the nasty Rottweilers he barely managed to restrain.

"Lemme tell y'all somethin'," he snarled. "Me an' Cleadus is always watchin', ya hear? If'n we ever catch ya slackin' we gives ya a dose o' encouragement with the lightnin' rod!" He patted the metal tube on his hip and continued to stare at the boys.

"Yer lightnin' rod?" Ploox mumbled.

"You heard me, Dumbo! An' from whut Ah recall ya already been through one 'lectrical storm! Ha-ha-ha! This here's a cattle prod, bigg'un, but fer my money it wuz custom made fer ridin' herd on rock rats like y'all boys. Ain't that right, Gonzalez?" As he spoke he spun about on one heel and locked eyes with Pepe, who had been painstakingly easing away from him.

The boy froze, and as Berfel narrowed his gaze, he began to quiver.

"Ole!" Berfel shrieked, and in that instant—like some deranged gunfighter of the old West—he drew his lightning rod and poised it inches from Pepe's nose. Then, with his free hand, he pulled a wad of work gloves from his back pocket and threw them on the ground. "Slip inta them gloves, you two. We wouldn't want ta damage them tender li'l hands, now would we? Naw! 'Cause then we'd have a drop in perduction an' we cain't have that. You boys jus' folla Gonzalez an' his partner over ta that stand o' cactus yonder an' we'll put ya to the test." He lowered the cattle prod, but he never stopped glaring at Pepe. "Gonzalez!" he screamed. "Lead the way! You need extra trainin' on a reg'lar basis."

Pepe moved out smartly towards a clump of prickly pear, followed by his chainmate. Ploox and Nicky Neill fell in behind them.

"Now, laddies," Berfel instructed in a sickening, sugar-coated tone of voice, "put a bend in yer backs an' make me a pile o' rocks. MOVE!!"

The four boys went right to work gathering up hefty stones, about the size of softballs, and tossing them onto a pile. But their efforts were soon interrupted by several sharp cracks from a long leather whip wielded by their fearsome foreman.

"Hey, you nitwits!" He stormed toward them. "Leave them pebbles alone! I want big rocks ... mansized!"

With a groan, Ploox and Nicky Neill hustled after the available boulders, scurrying around like a pair of squirrels in a forest fire. After a few mean jolts, they learned to work as a coordinated team, gathering and stacking stones like it was second nature. Spurred on by the thought of Berfel's lightning rod, not to mention his whip, Ploox labored at a furious pace. In spite of the glaring sun and soaring temperature, he strained and grunted like a wood-burning locomotive, dragging up one big rock after another. His performance became so impressive that the other prisoners started to chant, "Go, Ploox! Go, Ploox! Go, Ploox!" Nicky Neill smiled behind Berfel's back. Their torture session was turning into a morale booster, and that meant defiance of the system. After a minute or so, Berfel caught on and put a stop to it.

"Enough! Hold it, you coyotes! Ah seen it, but Ah don't believe it. You new boys is gonna work out fine." He turned away from them and wagged a threatening finger at Pepe. "As fer you, runt, ya better learn ta put some muscle inta them toothpicks you call arms ... or Ah'll jus' hafta find ya a new assignment. Somethin' permanent-like." Without wasting any time, he addressed the rest of the crew. "Awright, you buzzards! Let's git ta work. Make me two lines ... keep 'em spread. An' no slackin'!"

Like the old hands they were, the prisoners who had been standing by set about their customary task. No one looked up from his work, no one paused to wipe his brow or catch his breath. Because, roaming among them, lightning rod at the ready, shotgun poised, dogs straining at their leashes, was their beloved leader, Berfel B. Slack. And all he really seemed to be looking for was a reason to test his tools.

Nicky Neill was no different than the others. He was afraid to look up for long, if at all. Instead, he concentrated on working his hardest, praying that he would last through the day. For the time being, though, all that mattered was the moment at hand. He'd worry about the afternoon when it came ... if he was still on his feet to see it, that is.

CHAPTER 42

Several hours into their morning's labor, Berfel called a halt and ordered everyone under the shade tree. As they crowded in beneath the precious shadows he strolled among them, pouring relief from an enormous canvas water bag that had been delivered by Sweeney the Meanie.

"Here ya go, big boy," he grinned at Ploox, extending the swollen bladder in his direction. Ploox clutched awkwardly at the canteen, uncertain as to how he should manage to drink from it and hold it at the same time. He chose to embrace it in a bear hug and then hoist it to his parched lips. The life sustaining liquid responded to his grip and gushed from the spout, flooding his throat and bathing the rest of him. But he was oblivious to the waterfall he had created. Instead, he guzzled away like an empty camel at a desert oasis.

"Whoa, biggun! Whoa, I said!" Berfel thumped Ploox on the back of the head with a tin cup. It wasn't much of a blow, just an attention getter, but it sent the Rottweilers into a tizzy. "That ain't bath water, kid!" Berfel was snarling, but it was obvious he thought it was funny. "That ain't how we drink 'round here. Ya jus' hold 'er up to yer mouth fer a count o' ten an' then let 'er go. When ever'one's had a pull then Ah send 'er 'round again. Savvy? Ya hog-waller in it like that an' Ah'll see ya go without. Am Ah clear?" With that he ripped the bag from the boy's grasp.

Ploox nodded in reply, still gasping. When Nicky Neill's turn was up he crowded close to him and whispered, "Hey, how come he's so nice ta us all of a sudden?"

"Nice?" Nicky Neill asked, not sure what his partner was getting at.

"You know, givin' us water 'n' all. I didn't figger they'd give us nothin' ta drink."

"He's not being nice." Nicky Neill kept his voice low. "He's just doing what's necessary to keep us from keeling over with heat stroke. If we all dropped dead then they wouldn't have anybody to do their work. They just want to make sure we're still breathing tomorrow."

"Time's up!" Berfel announced. "Move out! I want ten tons 'fore lunch. Le's go! Ten tons."

For the next hour the boys worked at a blistering pace until Nicky Neill noticed everyone around them beginning to ease up. He figured that was a clue that lunchtime couldn't be too far away. But Ploox hadn't made the same observation. He kept right on chugging, fearful of Berfel's lightning rod and all the rest of his arsenal. He would have continued busting his butt, too, in spite of Nicky Neill's suggestion to slow down, had it not been for the occurrence of a curious event.

Ploox had just turned over a large, flat rock and was about to wrestle it into his arms when he spied a nest of scorpions exposed in the dirt. Tails raised, pincers at the ready, they scurried about in search of an intruder. Ploox had never seen a live scorpion before and they instantly hypnotized him. Nicky Neill ogled them for a moment, too, but soon realized their inactivity might attract some unfavorable attention. He was about to remind Ploox to get back to work when a shadow fell across his face. He glanced up to find Berfel tiptoeing behind Ploox. Before he could warn him, Slack levelled his shotgun at Nicky Neill and motioned him back. As the boy edged away he noticed that the dogs at Berfel's side were strangely silent now. Then, with all the precision of an artist about to apply the finishing touch to a canvas, Berfel stretched out his arm and guided the tip of that blasted cattle prod onto Ploox's unsuspecting fanny.

"Owwwww-eeeee!" Ploox snapped upright, straight as a board, and did a stiff-legged little dance around the fallen rock. "Ow! Ow! Ow! Owww-eee!"

"Don't act so *shocked*, sonny boy!" Berfel snickered, waving the cruel wand in Ploox's face. "Next time Ah plant this lightnin' stick on yer backside Ah'll leave it there a spell. Now git back ta work!" Berfel turned away and strode past the spot where Pepe was laboring, pausing long enough to deliver a quick jolt of punishment to his thigh. The prod crackled and the unsuspecting boy cried out in pain.

"Ai-yai-yai-yai-yai! Caramba! Why senor? Why you do thees? I'm working like a burro for you."

"Heee-hee-hee!" Slack revelled in his second surprise attack of the morning. "Jus' a reminder, chili pepper. So's ya don't fergit Ah'm watchin' ya. Besides, Ah like ta see ya do that little dance!"

While Berfel continued to chuckle at his ugly game, Sweeney the Meanie pulled up in the pickup and stuck his huge, bald dome through the open window. Every kid in that field shuddered at the sight of Sweeney's piercing eyes and threatening expression.

"How're them new recruits?" he called out to Slack.

"Not bad, Ev. Not bad a'tall. Mind you, Ah had ta give the biggun a nudge with muh stick."

"Whut fer. Wuz he slackin'?" Sweeney focused on Ploox, who was now working furiously.

"Naw, he jus' got all hyp'tized by a bunch o' danged scorpyuns. That's all." Berfel laughed at the recollection.

"Next time, kid," Sweeney wagged a finger at Ploox, "we'll let ya carry 'em around in yer pocket." Evrett shifted his gaze to Nicky Neill. "How 'bout the skinny one? He got anything goin' fer hisself?"

"He ain't bad neither, Ev. Matter o' fact, ol' Grady done right well by hisself this time."

"Hmmmph," Sweeney mumbled. "You keep on 'em, Berf. I'll be back after lunch with the dump truck. Looks like we got considerable loadin' ta do this afternoon."

"Roger that, Ev. See ya later." Sweeney departed in his usual cloud of dust. You could feel the tension decrease the further away he moved. Even Pepe seemed to relax.

Another half hour passed and the day burned on. Grasshoppers buzzed through the sweltering air in search of something green to gnaw, but the only green around had thorns all over it and skin as tough as leather. Cicadas, too, droned away in the thickets and their incessant whirring reminded Nicky Neill of home. But his bubble burst and vanished at the sound of Berfel's voice. "Bean time! Bean time! Shut 'em down, maggots. Ever'one under the tree. Pronto!"

"Come on, Ploox! Let's hustle! If we hurry we can lean against the trunk." As they made the dash a nauseating thought sabotaged Nicky Neill's joy. What if, he cringed, their lunch turned out to be recycled breakfast?

CHAPTER 43

*P*loox and Nicky Neill got lucky; they beat the rest of the crew to the shade. As soon as they arrived they plopped down at the foot of the tree. Seconds later they were joined by the others. Everyone was wringing wet, drenched in his own sweat, but Ploox and Nicky Neill's faces were redder than everyone else's. In fact, they appeared to be glowing.

"Salt time, laddies," Berfel sang out. "And it looks ta me like some o' you fellas is right on the verge o' heat pasturation. Make danged sure ya swaller all these pills ... an' watch how ya use the water." He was looking at Ploox when he delivered this last message. "Here, biggun. You first." Towering above them, he held out a clenched fist. His other hand offered the canteen.

"Uh, whut's this, Mr. Slack?" Ploox asked.

"Them's salt tablets, boy. Take yerself three of 'em an' wash 'em down proper. Then pass that water bag along." He watched as Ploox choked down the tablets. "Them'll keep ya from croakin' out here, 'less'n o' course ya wanna die an' shrivel up like a squished horny toad?"

Ploox was convinced. After he had downed his salt ration he guzzled a ten count of precious water and extended the bag to his partner. But Nicky Neill couldn't take it right away. He was busy reaching for his own tablets on Berfel's open palm. When he had scooped his share he turned to accept the canteen but Ploox had let it to sag beyond his reach. Nicky Neill was about to say something to him when he noticed his partner was mesmerized by something on Berfel's arm. His fixation quickly came to Slack's attention.

"What'cha lookin' at, kid?" he snapped.

But Ploox's eyes only widened. He was unable to answer.

"Oh!" Now Berfel snickered. "Ya done spotted Miz Lola!"

Ploox nodded and continued to eyeball the field boss's arm. By this time Nicky Neill had spied the object of his partner's curiosity and couldn't help but stare at it too.

At that very moment, Cleadus and his rock crew tramped into the area. Without so much as a word the new arrivals crowded into the scant shade and attempted to make themselves comfortable. Their boss proceeded to join his friend.

"Hey, Cleadie! Lookee here!" A wide grin spread over Berfel's face as he pointed to Ploox. "These two new pickers jus' fell in love with Miz Lola!"

"Zat right? Well, now. Maybe they oughta git ta see Miz Lola in action, huh?"

"Ah don't know, Cleadus." Berfel began to stroke his chin thoughtfully. "The sight might be too much fer their little pebble-pickin' hearts! On the other hand," he became all smiles again, "why not? Ya got yer juice box?"

"You betcha I do. Hang on!" Cleadus dug into his back pocket and pulled out a mystery package wrapped in a faded blue bandana. Unfolding the cloth, he produced a glistening harmonica. He slapped it against his palm a few times then raised it to his lips. When he blew into it a small cloud of dust and grit spewed out. "There!" He looked to Berfel and gave a little nod.

"Gentlemen," Slack began. "This here's a treat meant only fer fully growed men. But in yer case Ah'm gonna make an exception, seein's how y'all boys prob'ly ain't never gonna git ta be fully growed anyhow. Ha!" A serious expression suddenly masked his face. "But lissen, campers ... if'n any o' y'all gits embarrassed, why jus' turn yore little ol' heads! Savvy?"

Berfel stepped forward a few feet and looked Ploox right in the eye. "Git a grip on yerself, biggun, 'cause here she comes!" He began to roll his shirtsleeve up as far as it would go. What he revealed, in blazing color, was a sight the likes of which the boys had never witnessed. Right there, for all the world to see—occupying his entire upper arm, clear up to his shoulder—was a tattoo of a Polynesian lady wearing nothing but a wispy grass skirt and a smile. Luckily, for her, long, dark folds of hair fell across her shoulders and partially shielded her from total embarrassment.

"Hit it, Clead!" Berfel called out spryly, and his partner began to blow an old playground favorite. To the boys' complete astonishment, their foul field boss broke into song. "There's a place in France where the ladies do a dance ..." As he sang, Berfel flexed and unflexed his considerable muscle, causing the tattoo lady to sway back and forth as if she had come to life right there on his hairy bicep. The only thing missing was a palm tree.

CHAPTER 44

*L*ooking around that group of boys clustered beneath the tree it was obvious that not one of them had escaped Miss Lola's spell. But it was more than that, more than just the bawdy display of a raunchy tattoo. It was obvious, as mean and ornery as Berfel and Cleadus were, that they enjoyed making a spectacle of themselves. For a brief moment they let down the barrier that permitted them to treat the boys so cruelly. Clearly, it went against the grain of the Armadillo Ranch Camp philosophy. And it fooled Nicky Neill, too. Just when he believed he had found someone he could hate with all his heart, they pulled this stunt.

But then Berfel's performance came to an abrupt halt. For a second or two longer Cleadus played on before stopping just as unexpectedly. The two men stared down at the ground then lifted their gazes and peered off in a direction somewhere beyond the boys' heads. Following their look, Nicky Neill twisted around to see what had ended the show.

"Holy smokes!" he gasped. "Who is *that?*" Ploox was speechless again. His mouth had flopped open in disbelief and a tiny black bug flitted in and out of the gap.

There, behind all the weary pickers, mounted on a giant of a horse, sat the fattest, most peculiar human being Nicky Neill had ever seen. And perched right behind his saddle, in a snug little wicker basket, sat a bug-eyed Chihuahua pooch peering down at the world like some high and mighty Chinese emperor.

Nicky Neill felt his jaw drop too. How often do you see, up close and in person, a four hundred pound Humpty Dumpty look-alike? Whoever he was, his bald noggin glistened in the afternoon sun like a polished melon. A pair of dark, reflective sunglasses hid his eyes, and a mean little smirking mouth cursed them all without even moving. His mountain of an upper body was draped in a dazzling Hawaiian shirt. The tropical pattern of the material was so immense, in fact, that the rows of swaying palm trees actually seemed to move. His pants were made from a glossy snow-white fabric that billowed out like small clouds around the pockets and then tapered into tight pant legs that disappeared inside black stovepipe riding boots. From beneath the folds of his shirtsleeves, arms like elephant legs protruded awkwardly, smothered by avalanches of blubber. His hands, naturally, were fat and swollen.

For several long, uncomfortable seconds this human behemoth scrutinized the entire group. Nicky Neill glanced at Berfel and Cleadus and noticed how timid and nervous they had become. Whoever this guy was, his power matched his proportion. And then he did something that caught everyone off guard. In one deft motion, his left arm flew up from his side and he planted an odd-looking cap with a long, protruding brim on top of his gleaming skull. The cap reminded Nicky Neill of the head of a duckbilled platypus and every time Mr. Tubbo blinked he imagined an albino platypus winking out from his forehead. Then the man raised a sausage of a finger and pointed it towards Berfel and Cleadus.

"Mr. Slack! Mr. Hensley! Could you be so kind as to inform me how often you take it upon yourselves to entertain the troops in this fashion?" His voice was high, almost falsetto, but it was cold and threatening, too; an unexplainable anger seemed to boil beneath its surface. Like everything else about him, his use of language was strange as well. There was no twang to his accent. Instead, he talked like a sophisticated person, choosing his words carefully and deliberately.

"Uh, ya see, Mister ..." Berfel struggled with a reply. "Er, Ah mean, Master Rockford. We ..."

"Silence, you bumbling fool!" The rider was screaming now. "Hear me, and hear me well. This enterprise, *your* enterprise, is a business affair and NOT a vaudeville show for wayward street rats! If it is your desire to become performing artists, I'm certain I can get you a seat in the prison band! Is that CLEAR!"

Both men nodded that it was.

"Good." His voice lowered and returned to that sickeningly sweet, sugarcoated tone. "Now I shall leave you to your charges. I only rode out to inform you that the demand for your product has just been doubled. We have received orders for enough rock to make you both comfortably wealthy ... providing, that is, you can fill those orders. I suggest you expand your work schedule to accommodate the new business." He paused to survey the sea of uplifted faces. "Certainly these young ragamuffins are up to it, eh?"

"Oh, yessir!" Berfel's response was quick and confident. "They love the work. In fact, they're gittin' better ever' day!"

"Yes, yes. I'm certain that's true." The mammoth's reply was more of an absent-minded muttering. He was busy sweeping his attention through the sweaty mob below. "Tell me, boys," his little piggy mouth broke into a honest-to-goodness smile, "are you enjoying your stay at the Armadillo Ranch Camp?"

No one answered.

Then he raised one of those sperm whale arms and pointed directly at Ploox. "You! Tell me, is this your idea of summer fun?"

"Gulp!" Ploox swallowed, taking in the tiny insect that had continued to hover behind his teeth. "Uh ... no, sir! It's awful here! I'd rather jus' go home, if yuh don't mind?"

A broad grin rippled across the whole of that ample face, erupting into peals of excited laughter. He tossed his head back and continued to laugh with such uncommon vigor that it looked as if he might topple off his horse any moment. But he regained his composure long enough to speak again.

"Splendid! Splendid!" he crowed. Tears were rolling over his cheeks ... tears of joy. "They're having a *rotten* time! They would rather be home with their mummies! Oh, I love it! I love it, I love it! Slack! Hensley! Keep up the good work!"

Hysterical laughter consumed him again as he tugged at the reins and wheeled his mount around. Jabbing his boots into his horse's flanks, he set off at a brisk pace. Behind him the bug-eyed Chihuahua was yelping fiercely. As the fits of laughter continued he would mimic Ploox's reply: "No, sir! It's *awful* here! I'd rather go home. Ha-ha-ha-ha-ha-ha!"

Nicky Neill turned to the kid on his right and asked him, "Who is that guy?"

"That," the kid shrugged, "is Rockford J. Snodgrass. He owns the place."

"Owns the place?" Then Nicky Neill recalled what Alvin Dodd had said on their ride out. "So that's the millionaire, huh? But why is he a part of all this?"

"Because," the boy grimaced, "he hates kids."

CHAPTER 45

*E*veryone beneath the tree gawked after the tropical
island on horseback until the last swaying palm disappeared over a sun-baked slope. No sooner had he faded from
sight than an angry rumbling noise in the opposite direction
signalled the arrival of another visitor. The whole gang turned
as one to face the clatter. Moments later, Sweeeney the Meanie
wheeled his pickup alongside their oasis.

"Chow time!" he announced, scowling as usual. "Berfel,
you and Cleadus git over here an' pass this stuff out. I don't
want no more down time than's nec'ssary."

"Yeah," Berfel acknowledged, "we done got the news from
Blubberbutt. Time is money!"

The two field bosses moved quicker than they had all
morning. Together they hefted a large cardboard box off the
bed of the pick-up and carried it beneath the shade. Then they
leaned into it and began distributing the contents: bulging
paper sacks smelling of overly ripe fruit.

"Awright, ya li'l cowpies," Cleadus snapped. "See that
ever'one gits a lunch, an' make danged sure that all o' them
bags come back empty." He paused to let his warning sink in.
"Food's energy," he continued. "An' energy's whut y'all boys
need most. So eat up!"

In short order, every prisoner possessed a lunch sack and
was absorbed in the act of eating. Meals were one of the rare
luxuries afforded the residents of Armadillo Ranch Camp.

"Wow!" Ploox exclaimed, tearing into his sack. "Lookit,
Nicky Neill ... real food! There's milk ... 'n' juice ... 'n' fruit ...
'n' all kinds o' stuff!"

Nicky Neill probed his bag suspiciously at first, but there
were no tricks inside. Instead, he discovered a couple of ham

sandwiches; a package of Fritos; a pair of hardboiled eggs; two plums; a bruised peach and a speckled banana; two cartons of milk; a carton of grape juice; and three pieces of peppermint candy. But the reprieve from work was just as welcome as the grub. For a solid half hour no one cursed or threatened them, and the bloodthirsty guard dogs scratched out little beds for themselves in the dust and slept the entire time.

When Nicky Neill was done with his lunch he crumpled his trash into a tight ball and tossed it back into the cardboard box. "Ah!" he sighed. "That was a lifesaver!" Jack Watson had watched him sink his field goal. "Hey, Jack. How can this food be so good and breakfast such a disaster?"

Jack laughed grimly. "The cooks up at Snotty's own kitchen put these lunches together for us." He paused to make sure none of the field bosses were listening. When he continued his voice was much lower. "They believe we're honest-to-goodness campers. They fix our supper, too. But breakfast," and now he whispered, "is cooked up by Slack and Hensley." Jack rolled his eyes and pretended to jam a finger down his throat. Nicky Neill agreed with him and they shared a laugh. Then he watched Jack lean back onto the dirt and place his balled up lunch sack beneath his head. He was going for a nap! Nicky Neill eased back against the tree trunk and closed his eyes. Before he knew it he was asleep.

In what seemed like a lapse of no time at all, an awful racket awakened him. He parted one pair of eyelids and squinted towards the commotion. He observed Berfel and Cleadus unloading a pile of wheelbarrows from the back of the old Dodge.

"On yer feet!" Berfel yelled. "It's rock time again, maggots!"

Nicky Neill attempted to raise himself like everyone else, but something had happened to him. Every muscle in his body was knotted. As he forced himself off the ground a bolt of pain shot through him from head to toe. His back hurt so much he was afraid he might become paralyzed if he tried to straighten out. Then, right out of the blue, he began to feel light-headed and dizzy. "Ploox!" he cried. "Help!"

"Huh?" Ploox reached out and caught his partner before he went down. "Nicky Neill! You okay? Whut's wrong?"

"Oh, man, I don't know. My muscles are all tight and my head won't stop spinning. This work is getting to me."

"Well, can yuh make it?" Ploox's voice was frantic. "Should I ask one o' them bosses fer some first aid?"

"No, no! Don't tell them anything. Just help me up."

"Hey!" Nate Watson came to Nicky Neill's side. "I know what you're going through. Once you start moving again you'll be okay. Today will be the roughest." Nate helped Ploox keep Nicky Neill steady. "Just hang in there, whatever you do. If Slack knows you're hurtin' he'll make things even worse."

"Thanks, Nate." Nicky Neill forced a half-hearted grin. "I'll be all right."

"Okie-dokie, boys. Lissen up!" Berfel was standing in the bed of Sweeney's pickup. "We'll be mostly loadin' this afternoon. Startin' off, Ah want Jones an' Dixon in the dump rig, doin' the stackin'. Biggun," he pointed at Ploox, "Ah want you an' Skinny on wheelbarras, 'long with Burkett an' Schlinkman an' the twins. The rest o' y'all, keep on pickin'. Any questions?"

No one said a word.

"Good!" he went on. "The word is we work an extry hour taday, an' ever' day from now on. If ya got any complaints take 'em ta Mr. Sweeney. Ha! Awright, le's git a move on!" Berfel slid his straw hat back and scratched his forehead before another thought struck him. "Oh, yeah! Y'all boys in Hensley's crew, lend my gang a hand till Cleadus gits back with the dump truck an' the rest o' them wheelbarras."

CHAPTER 46

*L*ike a bad dream, the boys were at it again. The main difference between morning and afternoon was the level of misery. Now it was constant. Nicky Neill's muscles were so tight he hobbled when he walked and his arms kept on doubling up on themselves. His entire body was one big cramp.

And then there was the heat. The sun hung directly overhead and burned down like a blowtorch gone out of control. Ploox was in bad shape, too, but he was holding up better than his partner. While they waited for the dump truck to arrive, they gathered rocks with everyone else and managed to camouflage their crippled movements amidst the mass of prisoners. While they labored, Slack threw scraps of food to the monsters. Whatever he tossed them they caught in mid-air. Their naps had not dulled their reflexes.

Eventually the dump truck showed up and Cleadus's crew collected their equipment and returned to their original location. Then Berfel called Ploox and Nicky Neill over and instructed them in the use of the wheelbarrows. Their new assignment consisted in traveling from pile to pile, loading the assembled rock and then wheeling it to the dump truck. At the truck their task was to pass the stones on to Lawson and his partner, whose job it was to stack the load so that as many rocks as possible could be transported.

In the beginning, working with the wheelbarrows seemed easier. But once the barrows were filled, moving them became a backbreaking nightmare. To make matters worse, once the boys reached the truck every rock had to be unloaded, lifted up to the bed and shoved on board. After their first run Nicky Neill started to suffer in earnest.

"Ploox!" he heaved between breaths. "I don't know how long I can do this. My legs are turning to wood, they won't do what I tell them to anymore. And my arms are freezing up on me. I've got to rest."

"Nicky Neill!" Ploox's eyes reflected real panic. "Please! Ya gotta do it. I know ya can. If ya don't, Slack'll ..."

Just then, Berfel snuck up behind them. "Hey, you two! Whut's goin' on? Are you boys slackin' on me?"

"No!" Ploox spoke up. "No, sir! Uh, he jus' accident'ly swallowed a bumblebee! He's gotta have some water or he cain't breathe!"

"Whut? Swaller'd a bee! Ya pullin' muh leg, boy?"

Nicky Neill wagged his head that he wasn't and coughed feebly.

"Okay, okay! Hang on, kid. I'll fetch the canteen." Berfel spun around and dashed towards the shade tree.

"Whew!" Nicky Neill sighed. "That was quick thinking. You saved our necks."

"Here, skinny!" Berfel returned with the water bag. "Slosh some aroun' in yer throat an' swaller that dangnabbed bee. How'n the blazes that critter git 'n yer yap, anyhow?"

Nicky Neill guzzled the water and shrugged in response to Berfel's question. But he had a question of his own. "Excuse me ... gasp ... Mr. Slack ... gasp ... but how come the dump truck doesn't just drive up to each pile of rocks and let us pitch them in, instead of hauling them around by wheelbarrow? I mean, it seems to me it would be a lot faster."

Berfel narrowed his gaze and glanced around from side to side to ensure no one else was listening. "Look, kid. We do it this a way 'cause Mister Snodgrass, the boss, tells us to. So this's how it gits done, savvy? Now keep yer dad blamed trap shut 'n' put that 'barra ta work."

The boys did as they were told, but it continued to be a struggle. Each step, each movement, drew Nicky Neill closer to the ultimate limit of his endurance. He began to accept the harsh reality—it was almost over for him. Soon, not even

Slack's lightning rod could bring him back to life. Then Ploox stepped in.

"Hey, Nicky Neill," he whispered. "I got me a plan that'll help yuh make it through the rest o' the day. Watch!"

Ploox stooped to hoist another king-sized rock and wrestled it into Nicky Neill's wheelbarrow. But instead of laying it flat, he turned it on edge. He did the same with the next three stones, arranging them in a square. Then he wedged a wide rock on top of the others, like a roof, leaving a hollow space in the center of the pile. After that, he rounded out the load with smaller rocks, giving the appearance that the wheelbarrow was filled to the limit.

"Well?" he smiled. "Whutta yuh think? You load yer wagon as full as ever an' I'll do mine like this. Then we'll trade off. It'll be a lot easier for yuh to push this way."

"Ploox," Nicky Neill smiled, "I think you're getting smarter every minute! Thanks. This just might do the trick."

There was no break for the rest of the afternoon, but Slack did come around with the water bag and salt tablets. Thanks to Ploox's creative thinking Nicky Neill survived the ordeal. Still, it had been a tortuous—and nearly fatal—experience. And the next day would undoubtedly be a repeat performance.

After returning the dump truck for its third unloading, Sweeney reappeared with the big flatbed, the signal that the workday was coming to a close. No one wasted any time assembling back at the shade tree. From there, all wheelbarrows were loaded and stacked upside down in the center aisle. Then all of the prisoners climbed aboard and took their seats. As the engine sputtered to life Nicky Neill sank back against the railing and closed his eyes. He was so tired and miserable he was numb. The thought of passing out on that wooden bench and never waking up again was very appealing. But he knew he didn't have the energy for that ... dying would have required effort and he had none left to expend.

CHAPTER 47

With a truck full of dog-tired boys, the ride home was made in silence. When the rig swung into the barnyard it lurched hard to the left, spilling Nicky Neill and several others onto the wheelbarrows. While Nicky Neill struggled to regain his seat, he noticed that the truck had rolled past the barn door and on around the building to the backside. There, a tall windmill stood next to an immense stock tank filled to the brim with sparkling water.

As soon as the truck came to a halt Berfel killed the engine. The rest of the boys rose from the benches and prepared to file off. Ploox and Nicky Neill were the last two on their feet. Berfel appeared, pulled the ladder out and they all climbed down. On the ground, they formed two lines and waited.

"Awright! Awright!" Cleadus boomed, joining his partner. "Git ready ta wash 'em down!" As he yelled, he snapped his team of dogs to a long wire anchored to the earth. The wire ran along one side of the water tank. Nicky Neill watched as Berfel led his mutts to the opposite side and fastened them to a similar device. They were surrounded.

Then, from out of nowhere, Sweeney appeared, cradling a long, double-barrelled shotgun. "C'mon, c'mon!" he shouted, "Let's git this over with. I wanna git cleaned up muhself before dark." As an afterthought, he added, "Don't fergit, Clead ... we got us a poker game tanight."

"Okay, you two!" Cleadus pointed his lightning rod at Gonzalez and Gomez. "Le's roll!" With that, Berfel stooped to unlock their leg irons. As soon as they were free they peeled their clothes off and climbed into the tank.

While the first two prisoners attempted to wash the dirt off four more joined them. All the while, Cleadus stood by, screaming at them to hustle it up. When Pepe and his partner did climb out, they scurried around the tank like a pair of wet rats and picked up their boots. Then they formed a new line behind Berfel. When the line consisted of six laborers, Berfel led them around the corner of the barn and out of sight. Sweeney himself took Slack's place, waiting menacingly for six more dripping bodies.

Soon it was Ploox and Nicky Neill's turn. The water felt so luxurious they could have cried. Ploox's reaction was to start squealing. Instinctively, they both ducked under and swam to the opposite side. When they surfaced Hensley was ranting louder than ever. "Hey, you dadblamed tadpoles! This ain't no swimmin' hole! Wash up an' move on!"

When they didn't respond right away he approached the tank and raised his cattle prod. The boys took the hint and shot out of the water like a pair of flying fish. Minutes later, Berfel was leading them into the barn. He ushered them right up to their cell and waited while they stepped inside. Then the steel door slammed shut behind them and they were alone.

The cell block was cool and the stones beneath their feet were downright cold. A shiver raced through Nicky Neill's body but he didn't mind. He was alive.

"Mama!" Ploox gasped. "It's cold in here! Hey, lookit!" On their bunks, laid out nice and neat, were fresh sets of clean clothes. They wasted no time putting them on. Their next move, however, was the most rewarding of the whole day. Without a word they collapsed onto their bunks and passed out straightaway.

Before long their snooze was interrupted by the grating sound of tin clattering against steel. Nicky Neill forced one eye open and rolled over on his side, squinting towards the aisle. There was Cleadus, standing before the cell opposite theirs, running a ladle back and forth across the bars.

"Hit the deck!" he bellowed. "Chow call!"

Soon he was at Ploox and Nicky Neill's door making more of that same racket with his greasy scooper. "Come'n git it, dirtballs! This time Ah betcha there won't be no leftovers." With his foot, he pushed their trays under the door and continued his rounds, dragging the meal cart behind him.

The boys descended upon the trays like starving wolves and proceeded to inhale every morsel, right down to the last splatter. Through it all, Nicky Neill paused only once, and that was to remove a knuckle-sized bone that threatened to choke him. Without thinking about it, he dropped the bone onto his pillow.

When the boys finished eating they pushed their trays back under the door and plopped down together on the bottom bunk.

"Oh, man, Ploox!" Nicky Neill twisted his neck to one side until it popped. "I'm so sore it hurts to blink."

"Yeah, I know whut yuh mean. D'yuh think they're tryin' ta kill us?"

"I don't know. But if they are, they're doing a pretty good job of it. You know, if it hadn't been for you, I might not have made it this afternoon. How did you come up with that wheelbarrow trick, anyway?"

"Gee, I jus' did whut I thought you woulda done if I wuz in trouble."

"Well, I can tell you this. I know for sure now I made the right choice asking you to come along on this trip. No one else would have made it this far. And I'll tell you something else. We're going to get out of this funny farm. I think I have a plan."

"Huh? You got a plan ta git us out! Aw, man! I knew yuh wouldn't let me down." Ploox began to tremble with excitememt.

"Look. I'm not ready to talk about it yet, so just trust me, okay? By the way, did you have any bones in your dinner?"

"Yeah, a couple of 'em ... almost broke some teeth. Why?"

"Never mind why. Would you get them for me?"

"Okay, but yuh cain't do much with a couple o' little bitty bones." Ploox retrieved the scraps from his tray and handed them over to his partner. Then he paused long enough to say goodnight before climbing up to his bunk and collapsing. Seconds later he began to snore.

A short while after Ploox conked out, Berfel and Cleadus re-entered the cell block and collected the empty trays. When they had finished their job they lingered by the main door and surveyed the area.

"That's it, Berf. They're all bedded down fer the night. Le's git ... we're due at a poker party, don'tcha know!"

"Right, Clead. Lemme turn Trooper an' Annie loose. Ah'll be right with ya." Berfel stepped outside and returned with the two dogs. Unsnapping their leashes, he freed them and watched as they raced down the aisle, darting from cell to cell, making sure all their charges were in place. "Well," he slapped his hands together, "that's done. On with the show!"

A sharp series of clicks signalled the death of electric current for the bank of lights suspended from the ceiling. An inky gloom invaded the prison once again before the main door at the entrance swung open and Slack's contemptuous voice rang out in the shadows. "Nighty night, campers! Don't let the guard dogs bite! Ha-ha-ha!" With that, the door slammed shut a final time. Another day was done.

CHAPTER 48

*F*or several minutes a heavy silence enveloped the cell block. Except, that is, for Ploox's buzz saw snoring. Then a scratchy voice piped up next door. "Hey, Ploox! Nicky Neill! You guys all right?"

"Yeah," Nicky Neill answered, "we're okay. Tired as all get-out, but still breathing. Who's that?"

"S'me, Nate Watson. You guys did awful good for your first day out. But here's a tip. You gotta learn to pace yourselves, see? Stretch your energy so's you don't burn out by noon. Slack really doesn't expect any of us to go full-bore the whole day."

"Thanks, Nate. I'll remember that. Say, I saw you limping out there. You got a bad leg?"

"Aw, naw. Just a blister. I got me some new boots today and they're not broke in yet. You guys'll get new boots soon, I reckon. The hard part is getting used to no socks. Seems there's always some kind of sufferin' nippin' after you in this place."

"Say, Nate," Nicky Neill's words were more tentative now and he kept his voice low, "are those dogs really as vicious as they seem?" As he spoke his fingers brushed over the bones on top of his pillow.

"Mean! Hey, man, they'll tear your arm off if you stick it out there! Don't be foolin' with 'em. The big one is Trooper and the other one is Annie. Slack told us once they were trained special to hate kids. Believe me, they do!"

"Uh," Nicky Neill persisted, "did you ever see them actually bite anyone?"

"Listen, I seen three guys chewed up by Hensley's mutts! They carried 'em outta here in blankets. Said they was goin' to take 'em to the hospital."

"And?"

"An' they never came back. Don't ask me where they went. Lawson might know more than me. He's been here longer than anyone. But he don't like talkin' about it."

After a long silence, Nicky Neill spoke up again, this time in a whisper. "Nate, do you think it's possible to escape from this place?"

"You wanna know the truth?" he whispered back. "The truth is, no one will ever get out of here. The cons, they've been in prison themselves. They know what it takes to keep a man locked up ... an' we ain't but kids. But more than that, we're evidence, see? And Evrett Sweeney ain't never gonna let the likes of us put him back behind bars."

"Thanks, Nate." Nicky Neill had heard all he wanted to hear. "Guess we better turn in, huh? I'll see you in the morning."

"Sure. See you in the mornin'."

Nicky Neill fell back on his bunk and stared into the darkness. His thoughts roamed around the cell, but soon they drifted all the way back home to Waterville. He pictured his mom, Phin and Ellen, drawn up close around the kitchen table, worried sick. It was too painful to dwell on, so he turned his thoughts to Mexico and his dad. How would he ever rescue him when he couldn't even save himself? He shuddered. His own thoughts had become his enemies. Regardless where he turned, he felt threatened. Somehow, someway, he had to make good on his promise to Ploox and get them out of this nightmare.

CHAPTER 49

"Wakey, wakey, boys!" The taunting voice of Berfel B. Slack echoed over the stone floors and ricocheted off the walls. "Time ta fall out fer another great day in Texas! Ha-ha-ha! Now then," the trace of humor evaporated from his drawl, "drag them carcasses outta them racks an' stan' to fer brekfus."

Between fits of moaning and stretching, Ploox and Nicky Neill rallied their aching bodies to the call. In no time, the morning meal was behind them. After the chain-up drill all they had to look forward to was quivering heat, uncountable rocks, and another day that was destined to pass like a century.

Like a bad dream, they climbed into the big transport truck along with the rest of the prisoners. Fifteen minutes later their ride jolted to a halt and the real ordeal began. They took up exactly where they left off the previous day.

"Hey, Ploox," Nicky Neill whispered, bending low to pry up another stone, "why does it feel like we never left this piece of ground?"

"I dunno," he moaned, "but I dreamed o' pickin' rocks all night long. Then I jus' woke up tired."

That was the extent of their conversation for the morning. Talk required too much energy, and it parched the mouth. The boys had already discovered that rest was in scarce supply at the Armadillo Ranch Camp. As Nate Watson had mentioned on the ride out, the unofficial camp motto was 'slave and suffer' and the three brutes in charge did everything in their power to see that those words rang true.

The only thing Ploox and Nicky Neill had going for them on the second day on the job was that they knew what to expect. But leave it to Sweeney to foul up even that pathetic shred of security. It happened late in the day, close to quitting time. He decided he needed one more load of rock. So, for another two hours, both crews clawed the hillsides until the dump truck was overflowing a final time. But then he flew into a screaming rage because the load was unbalanced and the right rear wheel wouldn't turn. Lawson Jones and his cellmate, Junior Dixon, had to climb aboard and rearrange the entire pile. As punishment, Berfel and Cleadus advised them there'd be no baths that evening. Sweeney grunted his approval when he heard that piece of news.

CHAPTER 50

*T*ired, sore, and dirty, Ploox and Nicky Neill filed into the barn with the rest of the 'campers' and collapsed onto their bunks. In less time than it took for the boys to kick off their boots, Cleadus appeared on the cellblock, pulling the meal cart behind him. Berfel brought up the rear, his beloved dogs in tow.

"Here ya go, boys!" Cleadus sang out. "Beans 'n' cornbread. An' there's even some nuggets o' meat mixed in with them frijoles! Ha-ha-ha! Eat up, maggots, eat up! Jus' remember, this here's better 'n whut they fed me at Alcatraz."

"Alcatraz!" Ploox echoed. "Hey, Nicky Neill. D'yuh think he wuz really in Alcatraz?"

"Maybe. Anyway, who cares? He's not there now." Nicky Neill lowered his voice to a whisper. "What matters for us is that if you get a bone in your food be sure to give it to me, okay?"

"A bone?" Ploox's face wrinkled with the question. "Whutcha gonna do with a bone?"

"Sssh! Hold it down, will you? Don't ask me any questions right now. I'm working on a plan and I'll let you in on it real soon ... that is, when I find out if it's going to work or not."

As Cleadus slid their meal trays under the cell door, one of Slack's dogs took a vicious snap at Nicky Neill's hand when he reached down. He missed him by a good four inches, but the sound of those jaws slamming together made his heart stop. Nate Watson was right; those mutts were killers.

A few minutes later, Ploox sounded off with a satisfied burp and passed down his empty tray. It was so clean it practically sparkled, except for a small spot of ivory in one corner. It was a cluster of bones.

"Good work." Nicky Neill smiled up at his partner but Ploox never saw him. He had already flopped onto his bunk. In a matter of seconds he began to snore.

When Nicky Neill was done with his meal he pushed their empty trays under the steel bars and laid back to rest. Tired as he was, he couldn't allow himself to sleep just yet. He had to stay awake until everyone else was down for the night. Only then could he begin to work on his plan.

Before long, Slack and Hensley returned to collect the food trays. Afterwards, they made a final inspection of the cellblocks. Then, with the usual racket, they killed the lights and left the boys alone. For the next several minutes the only sound in the barn was the rhythmic clickety-clack of the dogs' toenails as they made their hurried rounds. Their duty done, they returned to their mat beside the exit and settled in for the evening. Nicky Neill rose up on one elbow and cocked an ear in the darkness. The prison was quieter than a tomb. In just a few minutes, he told himself, he'd give his idea a try.

The next thing he knew, something startled him into consciousness. One eye popped open and blinked warily. The air was blacker than Sweeney's heart. Still, he unhinged his other eye and rolled his legs off the bunk. While he continued to gather his wits he guided his hand beneath the pillow and wrapped his blistered fingers around a small collection of bones. "This better work," he whispered, "or I'll end up minus a couple of good fingers." He took a deep breath and eased himself onto the floor. From there he shuffled on all fours to the cell door. With his face pressed into the cold steel bars, he was able to make out the lay of the cellblock. He glanced up and observed the distant ceiling. Hundreds of tiny nail holes allowed pinpricks of moonlight to penetrate the gloom. It wasn't a flood lamp, but the moonbeams that filtered through the roof took the edge off the dark curtain.

In the distance he could make out the forms of the two sleeping dogs curled up together on their mat. If he didn't already know they were Rottweilers he'd have sworn they were a pair of black panthers. For all their murderous ways they may as well have been.

Nicky Neill summoned up his courage and his meager fist-ful of bones and poked his face between the bars. Very softly, he began to make a clicking noise with his lips. Before he could draw a second breath the bigger of the two beasts, the one known as Trooper, stirred and raised his huge head into the air. He was sniffing frantically. Then he saw Nicky Neill's face poking through the steel. At that same moment, Annie awoke and the two brutes sprang to their feet and raced towards the boy, who waited until the last second to pull his head back. As it was, he only managed to beat their arrival by a matter of inches. They were quicker than he had imagined.

For at least thirty seconds Nicky Neill faced the dogs, tak-ing care not to taunt them. They held their ground, glaring like angels of death, growling deeply, hungrily. Streams of foam and saliva ran off their bared fangs and spattered onto the cold stone floor. Then Nicky Neill began to speak to them. His voice was hushed but his words were kind and affection-ate. At one point he even thought about poking his hand out for them to sniff, but as he raised his arm they lurched forward in unison, snapping ferociously.

Nicky Neill's next move was to place both hands upon the floor in front of them. While they concentrated on his move-ment he rolled two of the small bones under the door. They leapt on the offerings and sucked up the meager scraps like so many cookie crumbs. Nicky Neill had two bones left. He repeated the gesture. Like before, they pounced on the scraps and devoured them. For a split second Trooper cocked his massive head at a curious angle and looked Nicky Neill over. No kid had ever befriended him or Annie before. Then he reverted to his old self, snarling and snapping alongside his mate, as vicious as ever.

"Good boy, Trooper. So much for lesson one." Nicky Neill peeled his eyes away from the dogs and studied the rest of the barn, looking and listening for evidence of anybody who might have awakened to observe his efforts. Grateful for one small success, he pulled away from the bars and returned to his bunk. In a matter of seconds he was dreaming of happier times and friendlier animals.

CHAPTER 51

*T*he following day, after their morning water break, Nicky Neill decided to let Ploox in on his scheme.

"Ploox," he muttered, stooping low over a blue-ribbon hunk of rock, "are you ready to hear about the plan?"

"Yeah," he whispered, swiping at his forehead. "Whut's goin' on?"

"I'm making friends with the dogs."

"The *dogs!*"

"Not so loud, huh?" Nicky Neill shot a glance in Berfel's direction. He was busy wiping down his bullwhip with mink oil. "Yeah, I'm feeding bones to the dogs. Last night I tried it for the first time. I think it's going to work out."

"Lissen." Ploox rose up and looked Nicky Neill square in the eyes. The expression on his face was one of near panic. "If this means I gotta git near them guys you can fergit it. I'd rather chicken fight with Sweeney than mess with one o' them dogs."

"Calm down. All you have to do is save a few scraps from every meal. That's it. I'll do the rest, and before you know it, we'll be out of this place."

"Okay, okay," he mumbled, getting back to work. "I'll save yuh some scraps. But how're them mutts gonna help us escape?"

"I'm going to make friends with them, for starters. Then, when we're ready to break out of this dump, they won't be there to chew our heads off."

"Wow!" Ploox smiled as he leveraged a hefty boulder away from the parched earth. As he stood to pitch it onto the pile he froze in mid- air.

"Nicky Neill! L-l-l-ook! Schlink's in trouble!"

"Now what?" Nicky Neill rose up and followed the arc of his partner's finger. "Holy Toledo! That's a rattlesnake by his leg!"

"Do somethin'!" Ploox dropped his rock. "Help 'im quick!"

"Freeze Schlink!" Nicky Neill shouted out. "Don't move a muscle!"

"Snake! Snake!" Ploox began to holler at the top of his lungs.

By this time Schlink had spotted the critter himself and was making like the perfect statue. He was too scared to run even if he wanted to.

"What in the blazes is goin' on here?" Berfel shouted as he ran toward the boys. When he caught sight of the rattler poised beside Schlink's leg he stopped hurrying. "Well, well, well!" he grinned. "Looks like someone got theirselves in a reptile perdicament!" He eyeballed Schlink in a mean, conniving sort of way. "Tell me, Mr. Schlinkman, you ever gonna slack off ag'in roun' me?"

"Nuh ... no sir!" Schlink gasped, unable to take his eyes off the coiled diamondback.

"Speak up, boy! Ah cain't hardly hear yuh."

"No, sir!" Schlink repeated, loud and clear. "I won't ever slack off again. Never, ever, Mr. Slack. I swear!"

"Please, sir!" Bobby Burkett began to plead for his partner. "Do something! If you save him I'll owe you forever. Honest!"

"Hmm," mused Berfel. "Awright, Ah'll save the li'l chicken liver. But first, he's gotta answer me a few skill-testin' questions." An ugly grin spread across his face as the rattler began to announce its intentions. "Who's the greatest foreman in the whole danged world?" With that, Berfel stuck his chest out and beamed like a proud parent.

"You are, sir!" Schlink replied in a heartbeat.

"An' who's the han'somest fella in all o' Texas?"

"You are, Mr. Slack!" Schlink was on the verge of tears now. "Please, sir! Help me!"

"Okay, kid," Berfel hissed under his breath, "you passed." He began picking his way towards the snake. A mere step or two away from the rattler he bent low and, in one lightning motion, grabbed the varmint by the tail and jerked it into the air. "Ooo-whee!" he crowed. "Look who's gotcha now, slither-stick!" Then the field boss began to dance about, dangling the writhing rattlesnake at arm's length. A wild, demented expression came over his face as he sang, "Ah don't like critters and Ah don't like kids, an' cain't nobody else do whut Ah jes' did!"

The entire work crew gathered around Berfel, horrified yet impressed by his display of courage.

"Hey, Gonzalez! How's about a li'l licorice whip fer some quick energy?" All of a sudden Berfel was moving towards Pepe. In an instant he was on him, waving the angry reptile a few feet from the boy's face. Then he spun around on one heel and started for Ploox. "Ploox! Ploox boy! How 'bout a pet fer yer pocket? Hee-hee-hee." He continued to head towards Ploox, taking short little hops as he went. But when he tripped over his own boots the snake passed dangerously close to his face. "See whut yuh done, biggun?" he cursed. "I'm gonna feed yuh a snake sammich, right now!"

Ploox threw his arms in front of his face and started begging. "No, no! Oh, no, Mr. Slack! I didn't do nothin'!"

Berfel paused and looked Nicky Neill's way. "I got yer pard-ner a tad scairt, Carpenter," he snarled. Then his eyes lit up. "Why, lookee, lookee! I do believe I detect a wet spot growin' in biggun's drawers. Hee-hee-hee!"

"Okay, fellas." Berfel straightened up and a serious expression replaced his air of depravity. "Enough fun fer now. Lissen up, 'n' lissen good, 'cause Ah'm only gonna say it once. Anybody Ah catch slackin' taday is gonna deal with Mr. Rattler here, one on one. So git back to yer chores an' don't lemme hear no bellyachin'. An' you, Skinny!" He looked Nicky Neill over from head to toe. "Ah want you an' yer pard ta hightail it up ta muh truck yonder an' fetch me a gunnysack under the front seat. Now go on, vamoose!"

When the boys returned with the sack, Berfel dropped the snake in straightaway. As he snatched the bag from Nicky Neill's hands he uttered a rare word of appreciation. "Thanks, sonny. Now git back ta bizness."

Once they were back to their area Ploox posed an interesting question. "How come Slack's keepin' that rattler anyhow?"

"Who knows? He probably just wants to scare us with it some more. On the other hand, he might want to take it back to the kitchen so the cooks will have something fresh for supper!"

"Gross! You think they'd really do that?"

"I don't know, Ploox. I wouldn't put anything past these guys. Then again, I hear ratlesnake meat isn't bad eating!" With that comment Ploox decided to let the matter rest.

At last, the word came. Slack ordered the troops to knock off and assemble at the transport truck. Day three was down and done. Nicky Neill watched Berfel, though, and sure enough, he loaded that burlap sack into the cab of his pickup. Maybe that poor critter would wind up on the menu after all.

Later that evening, after another meal of beans and two-day-old cornbread, Nicky Neill settled down to wait for his next encounter with the dogs. Like the night before, he passed out, only to reawaken when the pale moon had cast some of its silvery glow into their private darkness. And like the first feeding, Trooper and Annie gulped down his humble offerings with only a hint of gratitude. Still, he had scratched the surface. Somewhere along the way he knew he would win their friendship.

CHAPTER 52

*T*he days that followed at Armadillo Ranch Camp did not deviate much from the ones the boys had already experienced. They woke up early and went to bed exhausted. In between time they worked like slaves, plucking rocks from a hostile earth that seemed to grow a new batch every night. And Berfel and Cleadus never eased up on the screws. Still, the two of them were just wacko enough to make the drudgery occasionally comical. Sweeney the Meanie, on the other hand, hovered around the ranch like a bad dream. His mere presence was enough to intimidate everyone, field bosses included.

In the meantime, Ploox and Nicky Neill adapted to the gruelling schedule. Their blisters turned into callouses and muscles cropped up in places where they had never existed before. And with each passing night Nicky Neill drew closer to the dogs. The convicts celebrated their paydays with a big poker party every two weeks. As the eve of their next bash approached Nicky Neill was able to reach through the bars and feed Trooper and Annie by hand. They even allowed him to give them a few loving pats. This particular feat impressed Ploox, but it didn't make him any less fearful of the pair. Instead, he praised Nicky Neill for his efforts and let him know that when the time was ripe for their escape he would be right behind him.

The day before the bosses' poker party an incident occurred that almost put an end to the boys' sagging adventure. It was a blistering hot morning. The sky was cloudless and the air refused to yield the slightest hint of a breeze. It began with Pepe Gonzalez complaining about a toothache. At first, Berfel just laughed at him and invented a cruel stream of jokes to add to the boy's misery. But as the day wore on and the temperature climbed, Berfel became more irritable. Unfortunately, Pepe's complaints grew louder and more frequent. Finally, Slack had all he could take. In a fit of anger he drew out his lightning rod and marched to where Pepe was hunched over, moaning.

"Hush up with that bellyachin', yuh li'l jumpin' bean!" Berfel's teeth were clenched as he applied a jolt of current to Pepe's backside. "If'n yuh cain't knock it off 'bout that danged tooth, then by golly, Ah'll give yuh somethin' real ta whimper 'bout."

"Ai, maldito!" Pepe shrieked at the unexpected sting. "I cannot help eet, senor! Ees keeling me!" Before Slack could strike again, however, Pepe returned to work at a furious pace.

"Now that's more like it, Gonzalez!" The field boss was satisfied with the results of his handiwork. For him, the end always justified the means.

From where Nicky Neill was standing one thing was clear ... no amount of torture was going to fix Pepe's tooth. Every time he bent over his face registered an expression of pure agony. It was only a matter of time before his predicament became unmanageable. Sure enough, less than a half-hour later Pepe dropped the rock he was wrestling and let out the most anguished cry Nicky Neill had ever heard.

"Ai-yeeee! Ai-yeeee! Help me! Somebody, please help me! Ai-yeeee!" Nicky Neill twisted around to find Slack. He was glaring at the skinny prisoner.

"Gonzalez!" Something snapped inside Berfel, too. "You miserable li'l crybaby! Ah'll show yuh a thang er two 'bout *real* pain. Yuh want that tooth o' yers fixed? Well, don't go away, boy ... 'cause Doc Slack is makin' a house call. Surgery is whut Ah got in mind!"

Every picker stopped working when Berfel tied his dogs off to a mesquite tree. He then hightailed it to Pepe's side. With way more force than necessary, he threw their friend to the ground, pulled a pair of rusty pliers out of his back pocket and went straight for his victim's mouth. At the sight of those pliers Pepe screamed even louder. His pleas had no effect on the determined convict except to make him madder.

"Open that trap, kid!" Slack's voice rose above the din. "Open it up 'fore I bust it open!" Pepe realized Berfel meant exactly what he said. Tearfully, he dropped his jaw and a filthy hand shot in.

"That the one, boy?" Slack demanded.

"Ai-yeee!" Pepe screamed his response.

"Ah think Ah found 'er, gang!" Slack turned and snickered to the rest of the boys. "Now jus' quit yer squirmin', son. Ol' Doc Slack is gonna give yuh some relief ... free o' charge!" Berfel guided the pliers into Pepe's mouth and opened the bite.

"Nawww!" Pepe gurgled. "Wong toof!"

"Don't kerrect me, kid. Ah'll pull all of 'em if Ah have to!"

That was it for Nicky Neill. He couldn't bear to watch another second. A buzzer went off in his head and a little voice began to shout, "If you stand by you're as wicked as Slack." He started to run towards the two figures struggling on the ground only to be jerked down like a dog at the end of his tether. Ploox had not moved. Nicky Neill jumped up and shot a look at his partner that said everything. This was something that had to be done together. Their chain wouldn't allow it any other way.

Ploox's eyes met his partner's. Then he looked down at Pepe and Berfel. Nicky Neill picked up a length of chain. Ploox nodded and they began to run.

Berfel was unaware the boys were closing in. All of his attention was focused on the business end of those ugly pliers. With a slight twist of his wrist he gave a final yank and tumbled over backwards as the stubborn molar tore loose. As luck would have it, he toppled into the dirt at the same moment Ploox and Nicky Neill made their dive. When they collided Nicky Neill's head struck Slack's shoulder, knocking him flat. Gravity delivered the two boys on top of the field boss.

Ploox and Nicky Neill swarmed over him. All the rage, all the humiliation they had suffered the past two weeks, gave vent to itself in that one frantic moment. Nicky Neill planted his knees on Berfel's chest and cut loose with a volley of punches. Ploox, meanwhile, was bouncing wildly on Slack's stomach, trying his hardest to force the last breath of air from that ornery body. Then Ploox gasped, followed by a string of laughter as the air came to life with the snap-crackling sound of lightning!

"Aghhh! Aghhh! Lemme loose!" The dastardly dentist screamed and screamed again. Ploox just kept sticking it to him.

Over Nicky Neill's shoulder he could hear the other prisoners cheering them on. The enemy they were whipping belonged to everyone. Then a loud "KA-THUNK" echoed in Nicky Neill's ear and Ploox toppled to the dirt beside him. Nicky Neill twisted his head around to see what had happened, but all he caught sight of was a huge hand just before it clamped around his neck and hoisted him off Slack's chest.

In a spray of tobacco juice and thunder Evrett Sweeney drew Nicky Neill's face within inches of his own and roared, "What the hell do you think you're doin', boy! I'll learn you to hit a fully-growed man!" He began to slap the boy's face. The blows rained down so fast Nicky Neill couldn't keep track. Then the beating stopped and Sweeney slammed him to the earth and dropkicked him. Nicky Neill landed beside his unconscious partner where he collapsed, moaning, in excruciating pain. Through it all he could hear Sweeney bellowing, "What in tarnation happened here, Slack? Fer cryin' out loud, what happened, man?

Berfel was still confused, and humiliated beyond description. "I, uh ... I, uh ... look here Ev, I wuz jus' ..."

"Quit yer sorry mutterin', ya miserable jackass, an' tell me what in the blazes went down! An' stand up when I'm talkin' to ya. I cain't bear the sight of a man grovellin' 'round in the dirt like that." Sweeney shot a glance in the boys' direction.

"'Specially when it was a pair of pipsqueaks that put 'im down there!"

While Slack was attempting to explain the situation, Ploox came to, massaging a bulging lump at the back of his head.

"Awright! Awright! That's enough, Slack." Sweeney looked at the two boys again in a way that made them shiver. "You keep an eye on them runts, hear? That is, if yer still able to do yer job. In the meantime, I'll round up Cleadus an' his crew." As an afterthought, he added, "Be patient. I'll have to fetch the big boy, too. He won't wanna miss out on all the fun." Sweeney turned towards his pickup. As he departed, Berfel lunged for the shotgun that still lay in the dirt.

"Them two ain't goin' nowhere!" he shrieked. "Not if Ah kin help it!" He scooped up the weapon and opened the breech, insuring it was loaded. Satisfied, he levelled the double barrel on his attackers.

"No!" Nicky Neill yelled. "Don't do it, Slack!" Before anything could happen, Sweeney's forearm slammed down on the barrels and the gun exploded. Dirt and dust sprayed into the air five feet away from where the boys cowered.

"Berfel!" Sweeney's face was flushed red. "Git a holt o' yerself, man! Ya cain't kill 'em! We need 'em, hear me? We need 'em!"

Slack was still quaking and his breathing was labored. Sweeney grabbed him by the shoulders and gave him a firm shake. "What's done is done, understand? Now you best cool yerself down or I'll plaster yer backside with some o' yer own medicine. Got that? I mean it, this here's bizness."

"Yeah, yeah, Ah hear yuh," Berfel nodded. "But yuh gotta un'erstand how bad Ah wanna nail their hides, Ev. They bushwhacked me!"

"Look here, amigo," Sweeney wrapped one of his arms around Slack's shoulders, "I know what yer sayin'. But jus' wait a bit, huh? There's some things in this world that's worse 'n death, ya know?" He shot Slack a knowing wink. "Them boys'll wish they wuz pushin' daisies 'fore long."

170

Berfel began to smile. "Ah'm okay, boss. You go on ahead. Ah won't kill 'em like they deserve. Ah won't even bash their li'l skulls in!"

Sweeney was convinced his cohort had regained control. He gave the boys a final once over, walked to his pickup and drove away. Ploox and Nicky Neill watched in horror as the top dog departed. Their lives now rested with the one man who wanted them six feet under. But Slack didn't even speak to them. All he did was glare in their direction and shake his head.

Before long, Hensley arrived with his crew. The looks on their faces were not hopeful. While they formed themselves into a single line, Berfel approached Pepe and Arturo and unlocked the manacle around Pepe's leg. Then he sent Gomez off to join the rest of his cellblock. They were standing glumly by, helpless observers in an unfolding drama.

In spite of the granddaddy of all headaches, Nicky Neill could only think of what those demented convicts could possibly have in mind for them. What was there on this stinking ranch that might offer a torture worse than death? He had assumed that just being a camper filled that bill. He shuddered when he tried to imagine the sort of fate their twisted adult minds were capable of conjuring up.

CHAPTER 53

When the boys next saw Sweeney it was only for an instant. He arrived in a cloud of dust and guided his pickup to where Slack and Hensley were standing by. Beside him in the cab, taking up two-thirds of the available space, sat the humongous millionaire. Snodgrass, or Snotty, as the prisoners referred to him, just looked at them and smiled. While the pickup idled, Nicky Neill also noted the wooden boxes strapped to the bed. Whatever those crates contained had the dogs barking insanely and scratching at the cargo. Then the pickup chugged forward and rolled out of sight.

"Awright!" Cleadus announced. "Ever'one load up!"

As usual, the prisoners paraded single file onto the flatbed and took their regular seats. But this time Berfel joined them. Before he climbed aboard, he unsnapped the leashes on his dogs and allowed them to run free. Cleadus and his mutts bounded into the cab and they were off, rumbling along in the direction taken by Sweeney and Snodgrass.

The truck travelled across territory new to Ploox and Nicky Neill. Before long, they came to a stout fence. The gate had already been opened. They passed through and continued to chug along in low gear for several minutes until Cleadus killed the ignition and the flatbed coasted to a stop.

The field bosses wasted no time. No sooner had they stopped than they were ordering the troops down. When all of the boys were lined up they marched them towards a prominent hilltop. As they approached the summit Nicky Neill spotted Sweeney and Snodgrass leaning against their pickup. Some ten or fifteen feet in front of them a curious clutter of tin and wood littered the ground.

"Welcome, campers! Welcome!" The obese millionaire was beaming. As he greeted them he began to rub his beefy hands together in a gleeful display of anticipation. "What a distinct pleasure it is to see your shining little faces!"

Hensley herded the boys into a semi-circle on the far side of the mound of debris. Sweeney and Snodgrass remained where they were, opposite the rest of them.

"So," Snotty began anew, feigning a legitimate smile, "I hear there was a small rebellion today. Is that so, Mr. Slack?"

"Yessir, Master Rockford," Berfel mumbled in obvious embarrassment. His eyes remained glued to the earth and his feet.

"Chin up, my good man! Don't be so dismayed. The joy of punishment will redeem you!" Without missing a beat, Snodgrass shifted his attention to the boys. "Pay attention, peckerwoods! It's lesson time at Armadillo Ranch Camp." He then turned back to Slack. His voice took on a steely air. "And which lads, sir, are guilty of the vicious assault upon your person?"

"Them two, Master," he replied sheepishly, pointing towards Ploox and Nicky Neill. "Them two new ones. An' that scrawny li'l Mex'can started it all."

Snotty stepped away from the pickup and raised his hands to his ample hips. "So," he sneered, "it's the new boys, eh? My, my, I should have known. Discipline is something that must be learned. And today, kiddies, school is in session!" The man's tiny eyes fixed on the boys in question. Nicky Neill watched them begin to smolder, pig-like, in their swollen sockets. "Striking an adult," he continued, "calls for a very special punishment, wouldn't you say, Mr. Sweeney?"

"I agree, sir. But just what, exactly, ought that to be?" The way Sweeney answered him hinted that he already knew what Snodgrass had in mind.

"THAT," Snotty roared, "would be the RAT DIP!" Unexpectedly, he began to clap his hands and stomp about in the dirt in his rendition of a jig. "Bring the criminals forward, Mr. Slack, and let justice be served!"

Nicky Neill shrunk back. "The rat whut?" Ploox muttered in his ear. But the field boss was already singling the three of them out with the butt of his shotgun, pushing them around the edge of the junk pile towards the two bosses. They came to a halt in front of blubber butt himself.

"Now, Mr. Hensley," he sang out. "Fetch the boxes, please."

"Rat Dip! Rat Dip!" Cleadus sang and danced like a carnival clown as he made his way towards the pickup. "Dip 'em an' dump 'em," he shrieked. "Rats fer the runts! Zippety-doopda, it's a wunnerful day! Ha-ha-ha!"

Hensley removed the straps that secured the boxes to the truck bed and toted both of them to the mound of lumber and tin. With great care he lowered the crates to the earth and spun about for further instruction.

"Very good, Mr. Hensley," Snodgrass commended him. "Very good, indeed. Now, sir ... stand by."

CHAPTER 54

*B*erfel's dogs were working themselves into a frenzy trying to break open the mystery crates. Sweeney had to order Slack to chain them up again. While they were being restrained, Nicky Neill began to pick up on an eerie buzzing sound. He had heard that noise before. One thing was certain—the buzzing was coming from the crates.

"A big mistake was made here today, campers! There was a serious breakdown in Ranch rules." Snotty's voice rose in pitch as he drove his point home. "Attacking an adult, a field boss, in particular, is the single greatest error any of you could commit." He was carrying on at the top of his lungs now. "No one ever, *EVER*, may so much as look at an adult in anger at this ranch ... let alone *STRIKE* one!" Saliva frothed from the sides of his mouth. He looked like a human volcano about to erupt. It might have been funny had he not been so serious. Nicky Neill was beginning to fear they had changed their minds about shooting them.

Snodgrass was forced to interrupt his own tirade while he wiped the spittle off his cheeks. When he was done he diverted his wicked gaze away from the three boys and shifted his attention to the rest of the prisoners.

"Does anyone disagree with me?" His whole demeanor had suddenly changed. Now he was practically cooing.

Alvin Dodd raised his hand. "Huh?" Snotty's jaw dropped. "Put that hand down you imbecile!" But Alvin had made a committment, one he intended to keep.

"No, sir." Dodd kept his arm aloft. "I disagrees with you an' ever'thing else about this nuthouse outfit."

Slack was preparing to wade into the prisoners and mete out some justice, Armadillo style, when Master Rockford ordered him to halt. "Ah-ah-ah, Mr. Slack! Hold your ground for a moment. Allow me to engage this charming youngster in some frank and open dialogue."

Snodgrass asked Alvin to step forward. When he did, the world's meanest fat man proceeded to question him. "Tell me, son. Just what is it that you disagree with here, specifically?" His tone of voice was sickeningly sweet and laced with dangerous impatience. "Come," he continued. "Is it your hours of employment? Or maybe the style of your uniform? Perhaps you're disenchanted with your immediate superiors? Do speak freely, my boy."

Alvin didn't look around to assess his situation. He knew he'd put his head in the lion's mouth. He didn't hem or haw, either. He looked straight into Snodgrass's withering glare and said his piece in the same old man monotone he always used.

"What I disagree with, mister, is your lousy way o' thinkin' an' the fact that ya'll got a slave business goin' on in the twentieth century." Alvin paused to wet his lips. "An' them convicts you got workin' for ya, they ain't nothin' but stoolies. Yore day's gonna come, Jack. An' when it does, me an' all these other boys're gonna be there to pull that noose 'round your turkey fat neck!" When he said that the hilltop became so quiet you could have heard a pin drop.

For an instant, nobody blinked. Then the prisoners erupted in wild approval. The sultry air echoed with the sounds of cheering and catcalls until a blast from Sweeney's shotgun restored immediate order.

"Shut yer mouths, maggots!" he roared. "Or I'll pers'nally break ever' one o' ya in half with my own two hands!"

"Him! Him! I want *HIM*!" Snotty was screaming and jamming his finger repeatedly in Alvin's direction. "I want him! Bring him out! He'll swing with the others!"

Berfel plowed through a flank of prisoners until he reached Alvin, whereupon he knocked him to the ground with one blow from the back of his hand. In short order he unlocked the manacle at the boy's ankle. "Git over there with them others," he snarled. "Now!"

Snodgrass was still furious, so much so he could barely talk. But he managed to spit out a final order to Hensley.

"Prepare the Dip, Mr. Hensley! And somebody, get those despicable children ready!"

CHAPTER 55

Sweeney the Meanie stood by with his shotgun while Slack and Hensley pulled away the planks of heavy timber and hoisted the metal panels aside, revealing a dark, gaping pit. As soon as the final sections of tin had been withdrawn an unbearable, putrid stench arose from the hole. The four boys poised at the edge gagged in unison and stumbled backwards. The butt of Sweeney's weapon quickly blocked their retreat.

"Git back up there, varmints!" From the corner of his eye Nicky Neill noticed that both field bosses had rigged bandanas over their faces, outlaw style. Snodgrass cupped a fancy lace handkerchief to his nose. Evrett Sweeney, however, did not appear the least bit offended by the vile aroma. With his encouragement, the boys returned to the edge of the pit. While they coped with the fumes, Berfel and Cleadus went about their business.

Once the hole was exposed the two men dragged up a pair of Y-shaped tree trunks and dropped them, butt first, into pre-dug slots at either end of the pit. Next, they lugged a long, thick pole to where the four boys were standing and allowed it to fall at their feet.

"Now whut, Ev?" Berfel asked, somewhat perplexed.

"Dang it, Slack! Cover that hole up ag'in an' lay the pole acrost. Y'all know the rest o' the drill." Sweeney shook his head in disgust.

The two field bosses patiently replaced some of the wood and tin they had removed before stepping onto the timbers and hoisting the long pole onto the tree forks. The scene began to resemble a huge barbeque pit. A new wave of panic swept over Nicky Neill. They were going to strap them to that big spit and cook them to a crisp!

"Awright!" Hensley growled. "Mount up, cowboys! Step up ta that log there and straddle it, pronto like!" Ploox looked at Hensley as if he had a screw loose. "Whut, biggun? Cain't yuh see y'all boys is goin' fer a ride? This here," he gestured to the pit and the rigging, "is better 'n' any danged Ferris wheel. Har-har-har!"

"No! No, senor! Please!" Pepe begged. "Not thees!"

Sweeney stepped forward and rested the end of his gun barrel on Pepe's pant waist. "Kid," his deep voice boomed through clenched teeth, "you move up there or I'll ventilate ya an' then I'll tie ya ta that thing. Take yer pick."

Reluctantly, the boys moved to the pole and mounted it. No sooner had they taken their seats than Cleadus clambered up trailing a handful of rope. Soon Berfel was at his side. Together they set about binding the boys' ankles. When they were finished, each boy was snugly hogtied to the spit.

"Now," Sweeney instructed in a much kinder tone of voice, "take the lid off." His cronies were quick to comply, pulling the entire floor away beneath the boys.

Once again, an unholy odor ascended from the pit. Pepe, who was right in front of Nicky Neill, gagged and spewed his breakfast over the side. No one said anything, except the field bosses, who started cheering.

Then Snodgrass moved around to face the culprits. He edged to the lip of the hole and peered in. An ugly smile rippled across his face. "The rats, Mr. Hensley!" he announced. "Dump the rats!"

"Comin' up, boss!" Cleadus hooted. The boys all turned their heads to watch him lift one of the mystery crates and give it a violent shake. Then he shuffled as close to the edge of the pit as he dared and pried up a corner of the lid. "Adios, snake bait!" he sang out, and emptied the contents of the box over the side.

With a terrible screeching and scratching, a furry gray cluster of squirming rats tumbled out of the box and somersaulted into the shadows below. As they impacted a new commotion began. The overriding noise was a loud, monotonous buzzing, a dizzying drone that soon filled the air. The racket reverberated off the walls of the pit until the only thing the boys could hear was the maddening hum of that death-infested hellhole.

"Hensley!" Snodgrass snapped his finger. "The rest of the ammunition, please!"

Cleadus pried the lid off the remaining box and tilted the opening towards the hole. A ball of rattlesnakes rolled out, all sluggish and heavy, and disappeared into the depths. As they joined their brothers below the noise level increased. And the fear factor quadrupled.

At last, Nicky Neill lowered his eyes and stared into the murky abyss. "Oh, Mama!" He recoiled in shock. "It's all over now!"

Seven feet below them the floor of the pit was a writhing, raging landscape. Thirty or more rattlesnakes littered the earth. And all around them, scurrying for their lives, were the rats. Carcasses of fallen rodents were strewn among the vipers, many of which were coiled, ready for their next strike. Some of the biggest rattlers slithered across the floor in more aggressive fashion, seeking out the prey of their choice.

"Hey, Carpenter!" Berfel called from the rim. "See anyone yuh know down there?"

"Whut's he talkin' 'bout?" Ploox's voice was faint, barely a whisper. Nicky Neill twisted around to see him. His eyes were sealed shut and he was attempting to breathe as little as possible.

"You don't want to know. Just keep your eyes closed like they are now. You're better off that way."

"Come now, lads!" Snodgrass spoke up. "It's time to pay the piper. To show you just how generous I can be I'll tell you what I'll do. If you four live through this my employees and I will welcome you back to the Ranch, with clean slates and all the privileges that go with being a camper! Sound fair? Ha-ha-ha! Mr. Hensley! Rotate the rascals, if you please!"

CHAPTER 56

C leadus was quick to act on Rockford's order. He moved directly to the end of the pole nearest Pepe. "Tell them diamondbacks 'bout yer toothache, chili pepper!" he said. Then he wrapped his meaty hands around the log and gave it a violent twist. The pole rotated and the four boys spun upside down.

"Whoa! Mama!" Ploox screamed.

"No, no, no, no!" Pepe pleaded.

The twist of the pole sent the boys flying headfirst into a wretched semi-darkness. They all threw their hands out in a reflex to break the fall. But they didn't smash into the bottom of the pit. Instead, they snapped to a painful hover and dangled above the carnage. The ropes at their ankles secured them to the log, guaranteeing a slight margin of safety.

"Madre mia!" Pepe moaned. Then his whole body went limp. His arms flopped beneath him, extending just beyond the reach of a huge rattler who was striking out in every direction.

"Oh, man!" Nicky Neill reached for Pepe's arms to pull him away from the danger but he could not quite seize him. "Ploox! Give me a hand here. Push me forward so I can grab hold of Pepe."

But Ploox didn't respond.

"Ploox! What's wrong with you? Give me a push! Now!"

"Hmmn," Ploox groaned. He sounded sleepy. "I cain't open muh eyes. I'm too scairt!"

"You open your eyes right now, George Plucowski! Or this kid's going to die!" Seconds dragged by. Then Nicky Neill felt Ploox's big hands pressing against his shoulders. It was enough for him to latch onto Pepe and lift his arms clear of the danger. "Thanks. I think we got him in time."

181

"Are they gonna leave us here, Nicky Neill? Arggh!" Ploox gagged on the fumes. "Tell me they ain't gonna leave us here."

"No! They won't keep us here for long. Too much work to do. They need us." Nicky Neill had to stop talking. A throbbing sensation began to intensify in his head. He'd never hung upside down for longer than a few seconds. Then he thought about Alvin. "Alvin! You okay?"

"Yeah," he answered slowly. "Lawdy, I hate snakes!"

A taunting voice from above interrupted their terror. "Oh, boys!" It was Snotty. "Oh, boyyyys? I've gathered your little hoodlum friends around the hole with me. They're all beside themselves with worry! But don't you find this little 'dip' is doing you a world of good?"

Nobody answered him.

"Come now, lads, don't be disrespectful. Talk to me! That is, if you're still alive down there! You know, it would be to your advantage to beg my forgiveness."

Still, no one offered a response. Nicky Neill began to rack his brain. Snotty was undoubtedly invoking some deranged brand of psychology. Nicky Neill knew he had to say something to him. Otherwise, they might hang out in that cesspool until dark ... or longer.

"Tsk, tsk, tsk. Stubborn little jellybeans, aren't we? In that case, another ten minutes will be so character-building!"

"Noooo! Huh-uh!" Ploox began to wriggle strenuously. Somehow, in a frenzied effort, he caught hold of one of his pant legs. From there he pulled himself upright, even with the log.

"No, Ploox!" Nicky Neill implored him. "Stop!" But Ploox kept on climbing, applying all of his formidable strength. In seconds he had managed to haul himself back on top of the pole, into the clear, clean air of daylight.

But his escape didn't last long. One of the foremen stood ready with a whip. A hard rain of popping leather sent him hurtling back into the pit.

"Aggh!" Ploox screamed in utter frustration. "I hate you guys! Hear me, Slack? I hate yuh!"

CHAPTER 57

*A*nother ten minutes passed before the tortuous silence was broken by Rockford's bogus sweet voice. But it was harder for Nicky Neill to listen to him this time because of another distraction. The rope that bound his ankles was cutting its way through his skin, choking off the circulation to his feet. His head was throbbing, his ankles were burning, his feet were numb, and the putrid fumes that he was forced to inhale were beginning to have an unpleasant anaesthetic effect on him. He kept passing out for two and three seconds at a time. He was certain Ploox and Alvin were sharing the same experience.

"Oh, pit divers! How about it, scum sniffers? Have you decided to speak up yet?" Snodgrass paused, hoping for a response. When none arose he continued. "Here's a little hint for improving your lot. You just guess what the magic password is and I'll have you delivered from your basement suite! Deal?"

Magic password? Nicky Neill thought. What *is* this pinhead talking about? Then, in spite of his muddled brain, it dawned on him. Coming from Snodgrass it could only mean one thing. "Ploox!" he hissed. "Alvin! I think I know what Fatso wants to hear. So I'm going to tell him, but I want you guys to know I don't mean a word of it. Okay?"

"Shore, Nick," Alvin groaned. "You tell that sucker anything you need to. Jus' git us outta here."

"Yeah," Ploox grunted. "Do it! Jus' do it!"

Nicky Neill craned his head back and cleared his throat. "Master Rockford, sir!" he began. "May we please be allowed to come up? We've learned our lesson." He blacked out then because the next thing he recalled was his neck snapping to and fro and a crazy quilt of stars and colors exploding behind his eyes. He took up where he thought he'd left off. "We apologize for hitting an adult, sir! We'll never ever do such a thing again. Honest!" He paused to catch his breath and swallow. Then he mustered the last reserve of energy he possessed to finish his plea. "Please forgive us, kind Master, Rockford the Great! We understand now about discipline."

Bobby Burkett told Nicky Neill later that a genuine smile spread across Snotty's face when he heard the boy's appeal.

Still, Snodgrass allowed the tension to mount. Finally, he gave the word to the field bosses. "Okay, men! Bring the little beggars out."

Still upside down, the boys found themselves rising into the air. The stench from the pit grew fainter as they cleared the shadows. Nicky Neill dropped Pepe's arms and looked beyond his limp body. There he saw Sweeney, cradling the pole over one of his massive shoulders, hoisting them away from that wretched crater. Berfel and Cleadus were on the other end working together. With a mighty heave the men dragged them over the lip of the hole and deposited them, pole and all, at Snotty's feet. Pepe regained consciousness when his head caromed off the soft dirt.

"Welcome back to the world of the living, boys! How was it down there in Hades?" Snodgrass rocked back on his heels and chuckled to himself. "Now that you've consorted with the serpents I'm certain you'll be anxious to experience my next punishment, eh? Just understand this." He leaned down and scrutinized their faces. "The next time, I won't allow you the luxury of a mere dipping. The next time we'll throw you in, secure the lid and let you fend for yourselves! Ha-ha-ha! Remember," he wagged a sausage-like finger at the rest of the prisoners, "it's a sin to be young and irresponsible. Thanks to me and my assistants you boys are learning the value of hard work and discipline. One day, should hell freeze over, you will become respectful citizens of this fine state. So, just do as we tell you and you will enjoy your camping experience. Break the rules and, as you see, you will be reckoned with. Now, does everyone understand?"

Twenty-two heads bobbed up and down as one.

"And," his gaze narrowed on Alvin, "does anyone disagree with me?" This time, no one moved a muscle. "Good, very good then! Consider your lesson over. Mr. Slack! Mr. Hensley! Away with them! I've had enough of children for one day. Any more of them and I won't be able to enjoy my dinner."

That was the end of it. Snodgrass climbed into Sweeney's pickup and together they departed the area. As for the prisoners, they were escorted back to the picking fields. Lunch was not served that afternoon.

CHAPTER 58

"We shore 'nuff showed them lizard lickers a thang er two 'bout authority, huh Berf?" Cleadus grinned in the boys' direction as he thumped the cell door with the butt of his shotgun.

"Yeah, Ah reckon. But fer the life o' me I still cain't figger how them two got on top o' me. I shoulda wrung their necks fer whut they done, an' I might yet." Slack stepped up to the bars and pressed his ugly mug against the steel. "Yuh hear whut I said, skinny? Ol' Berf's on yer tail now. One more goof-ball move like taday an' y'all boys kin kiss this world goodbye. I'll sic muh dawgs on yuh next time."

Nicky Neill pulled back to the darker shadows near the foot of his bunk and plugged his ears. But he could still hear Berfel's surly voice.

"An' another thang," he went on, walking away. "If'n it wuddn't fer Sweeney bein' so all-fired concerned 'bout you runts workin' tomorruh, Ah'd o' pitched yer suppers in the trash." He finished his last remark as he prepared to step through the big door. Before he departed he unleashed his dogs. Then he was gone. Cleadus followed after him, pausing long enough to switch off the lights.

"Neeky Neill," Pepe called out. "Sorry you guys make such bad enemies today because of me."

"Don't sweat it, amigo. Besides, we were never his buddies to begin with."

"Hey!" Jack Watson joined in the conversation. "Was it worth it, you guys?"

"Well," Nicky Neill said, smiling to himself, "when Ploox and I were on top of him it sure was. And when Ploox zapped

Slack's hairy belly I never felt so great! Don't ask about the Rat Dip, though."

Then, with a terrible bang, the main door flew open and Berfel's head poked through. "Ah thought Ah told y'all road apples no more talkin'! Now shut yer mouths an' git ta sleep 'fore Ah come over an' wire 'em closed." All talk died out on the spot. Seconds later, the door slammed shut again. This time, nobody said a word.

Nicky Neill lay on his bunk and stared into the darkness. Eventually, he stood up on the edge of his mattress and gave his partner's shoulder a gentle shake. "Wake up, Ploox," he whispered.

"Huh? Zat you, Nicky Neill?"

"Yeah, it's me. Relax. We need to talk."

"We do? Ain't it the middle o' the night?"

"Yeah, it's late all right, but I can't stop thinking about what Slack said."

"Yuh mean the part 'bout him bein' on yer tail? Do yuh think he's after me, too?"

"Hey," Nicky Neill stifled a laugh, "you're the one who was trying to electrocute him! He's on your case as much as mine. We're in this thing together. It's us against them, and I don't like our chances. Next time something breaks we might not be so lucky. I don't plan to die here, do you?"

"Die!" Ploox gasped. "They wouldn't really kill us, would they?"

"They came pretty close today, wouldn't you say?"

"Uh-huh."

"Look," Nicky Neill continued, "I don't plan on sticking around here much longer. We've got to get out, and the sooner the better ... while we still can."

"Yeah," Ploox's voice lowered, "but I don't want 'em to catch us tryin' to escape. Jus' think whut they'd do to us then!"

"Listen, Ploox, you need to remember something about today: you were a hero. You stood up to those guys like a real man. And you took their lousy punishment, too. Look around this place. Most of these guys have given up. Their spirits are broken. Once that happens any hope for escape sails right out the window. Don't you see, it's up to us to make the move. Not just for you and me, but for everyone.

"But I'm scairt! Real scairt!"

"We're all scared, Ploox. But that's not going to stop us. The next time we take a stand we'll beat those guys, I swear."

"Okay, Nicky Neill. If you say so. Have yuh got yer plan worked out yet?"

"Yeah, as a matter of fact, I do."

"No kiddin'! Whut is it? Tell me!"

"Okay," Nicky Neill whispered, "bring your ear over here." Ploox hunkered down as close as possible. "Did you ever notice that one stone under our cell door? The long one that tilts a little bit every time you walk on it?"

"Yeah! I felt that one jiggle!"

"Okay, half of that sucker runs into our cell. The other half pokes into the aisle. If we can somehow pry that baby up and pull it out of there, we might be able to crawl under the door. What do you think?"

"Oh, no! I ain't goin' out there with them dogs. No way!"

"Take it easy, pal. I'll do the outside work with those two. They're eating out of my hand now."

"Huh! Come on, don't kid me 'bout that."

"All right, then. Watch this." Nicky Neill stepped down from his bunk and fished under his pillow for the scraps they had saved. "Well! Come on. You can't see anything from up there."

Nicky Neill dropped to his hands and knees and Ploox followed after him. When they reached the bars of the cell door he smacked his lips a few times and held his arm out. In a flash, the dogs were there, licking and slobbering all over him. Ploox was speechless.

CHAPTER 59

"*P*lucowski!" Berfel screamed from a distance. "Git crackin' over there 'fore Ah rupture that butt o' yers!"

"Yessir!" Ploox responded without looking up. He was already working as hard as he could.

"Hey, Carpenter! You skinny sapsucker! Them rocks better fly, er this here bullwhip is gonna have a taste o' yer hide! 'Course, yuh know how Ah'd hate ta do that ta such a nice kid! Ha-ha-ha!"

"Boy howdy," Nicky Neill grumbled, "he's not going to let up, is he?"

But Ploox never answered him. He had just turned over a mountain of a rock. Beneath it something riveted his attention. Two rusty objects lay embedded in the dirt. He glanced around to make sure he wasn't being observed, and then he scooped the items up and jammed them into his pocket.

Nicky Neill watched his friend complete the maneuver, but he continued working as if nothing had happened. Whatever he had found would have to be smuggled into the barn. A few minutes later he noticed Ploox edging behind a clump of weeds. He knelt down to retie a shoelace. As he did, he pulled his earlier discoveries from his pocket and stashed them inside his boot. Before Slack's watchful eye could detect anything he was back at work, laboring harder than ever.

That evening, after the dinner trays had been collected, Ploox called down from his bunk. "Nicky Neill, I got somethin' for yuh. Maybe it'll help yer plan." Straightaway, he slid over the edge and joined his partner below.

"So," Nicky Neill wrapped an arm around his shoulder, "what have you got in your boot?"

"Huh? How'd ya know 'bout that?"

"I was the only one who saw you, believe me. Come on, what is it? I've been waiting all day for this!"

Ploox untied his work boot and eased it off. After he placed it on Nicky Neill's bed he dipped his hand inside and seized his prizes. A faint metal jingle echoed as he retracted his fingers. "Here!" he said. Nicky Neill scraped the objects off his partner's palm and began turning them over in his own hand. He recognized them by touch.

"Wow! Ploox! You are too much!" What he had managed to smuggle past the bosses was a long rusty nail and an old door hinge. "These are exactly what we need for digging that rock out." Nicky Neill hugged his partner. "You know, someone up there must like us!"

"So," Ploox heaved a thankful sigh, "when do we start?"

"Tonight! We're busting out tonight! I figure there's nearly a full moon coming up. We better make use of it."

"Tanight? But ... but ..."

"No buts about it. We can't afford to wait. Besides, this is the bosses' big poker night. You heard them talking. If they get as drunk as they say they will they won't be as likely to come down here and mess with us. Remember Leon? Let's just give them some time to drink up and then we'll get to work."

"Nicky Neill!" Ploox grabbed his friend's arm. His voice tingled with excitement. "I wuz thinkin'. That there rock under our door might be the last one we ever hafta lift!"

"Ploox," Nicky Neill's smile almost lit up the darkness, "that's the finest thought I've had all day!"

CHAPTER 60

*T*he boys lay there on their bunks staring into the darkness for hours. Once the decision had been made to
carry through with the breakout there wasn't much call to talk.
Finally, a loud commotion from the bosses' cabin signalled the
time had come for them to begin.

"Sounds like the game is underway, huh?" Nicky Neill gave
Ploox's bunk a nudge with the toe of his foot.

"Yep, sure does. If booze does ta them guys whut it did ta
me an' Leon, they won't be no trouble at all."

"Right!" Nicky Neill rolled out of bed. "Let's get to it."
Ploox slid from his mattress to join him. As Nicky Neill went
about collecting the tools and food scraps, his partner
remained close behind him, pressing into his backside like an
overweight shadow.

"Hey!" Nicky Neill twisted around to face his friend.
"What's with you? I can't work if you're leaning on me!"

"Aw, sorry," he giggled. "I jus' wanna ask yuh 'bout them
other guys."

"What about them?"

"They're gonna hear us, ain't they?"

"Probably, but so what? It doesn't matter anymore. If they
want to stay up and listen to us dig that's okay by me."

"Yeah," Ploox sighed, withdrawing to a normal distance, "I
guess yer right."

"Okay, give me your hand." Nicky Neill pressed the hinge
into Ploox's palm. "You start to work on the section of rock
inside the cell. I'm going to feed the dogs what scraps I have
left. Then I'll start digging on the end outside."

The dogs were standing by, waiting anxiously. Nicky Neill
snaked his arms through the bars and dropped their snacks

beside the loose stone. While they lapped up the tidbits he began to chip away at the mortar with his nail. But Trooper and Annie inhaled their morsels and turned to him for more. They demanded attention, slobbering over his hands and face with a puppy-like vengeance.

"Whoa! Easy guys!" Nicky Neill pulled back into the cell to catch his breath. "Okay, I'll give you some loving, but then you have to let me work. Deal? Yeah!" He scratched their ears and massaged the loose skin up and down their scalps. "Good dogs. You need love too, don't you? Okay now, sit down there and behave yourselves. Go on, sit!" Like the obedient mutts they were, they slumped back on their haunches and waited for the next command.

Nicky Neill went back to breaking up the mortar. He was stabbing away at the crack for all he was worth when a voice called out from across the aisle. It was Lawson Jones.

"Whut's you two fools doin' anyway?" he said. "Y'all boys is tryin' to dig outta here, am I right?"

"That's right," Nicky Neill answered.

"Y'all cain't do that. No way!" Lawson spoke with unconcealed scorn.

"We'll see about that."

"Hey, Nicky Neill!" Nate Watson joined in. "Where are the dogs? How come they ain't rippin' into you?"

"He's been feedin' 'em," Lawson piped up. "I been seein' it all along. He done made frien's wi' them debbils."

"No kidding?" Nate was impressed.

"What about the rest of us?" Skeeter Wilson joined in from next door. "You guys ain't jus' gonna leave the rest of us behind, are you?"

"We'll worry about that once we get out of our cell," Nicky Neill replied.

"Well, say!" Ploox spoke up. "Why d'yuh care 'bout this now? None o' yuh wuz too keen on escapin' before. Are you guys all of a sudden sayin' yuh wanna come with us?"

"Yeah! Sure!" A chorus of voices rang out in the shadows.

" 'Member what Sweeney said," Lawson warned. "There's worse'n the Rat Dip. Any o' y'all git's caught at this game, them bosses gonna smoke yore asses. You be dead campers 'fore supper, sho 'nuff."

"So what!" Skeeter shot back. "Ain't no way I'm bein' left behind in this dump. I'll take my chances on the outside."

"Look you guys! Let's not argue about it now. Everybody needs to keep their mouths shut while we finish our digging. If you want to help us, keep a close listen for any noise that sounds like someone coming. If we get caught in the act me and Ploox are done for."

All discussion ceased on the cell block. Even Lawson held his tongue. Instead, the rest of the prisoners turned their attention to the steady stream of racket coming from the field bosses' cabin. Ploox and Nicky Neill concentrated on loosening the stone. Every so often Nicky Neill would pause to rake in the debris he had dug up. Beyond that, they never let up or gave much thought to the convicts.

Some time later the boys heard a loud exchange of shouting and swearing followed by the bang of a screen door slamming shut.

"Someone ain't too happy up there," Hank Evans announced.

"Ssssh! I think someone's comin'!" warned Alvin.

Everyone scrambled for his bunk, including the two diggers. All the while, Nicky Neill prayed that whoever was on his way to the barn wouldn't notice what they had been up to. In a matter of seconds, Sweeney the Meanie flung the barn door aside and staggered through the opening. The pungent, nauseating odor of liquor followed him in like sour aftershave.

"Awright, ya little maggots!" he roared. "I jus' wanna ... hic! ... tell ya one thang ... hic! I HATE EVER ONE O' YA! Y'all ... hic! ... hear that? I'm sick an' tired o' playin' nursemaid." He stopped shouting and began fumbling about for the light switches. "Awwww, hang it! Jus' go an' have a nightmare, will ya!"

While his words echoed in the darkness, he reeled back outside and kicked the door closed behind him. Then the boys heard him trip and crash to the ground. He cursed a blue streak and gave the door a final kick before picking himself up and scuffling back to his cabin.

"I think ol' Sweeney musta lost tonight," a relieved Watson brother sighed.

"Yeah," someone else added. "And it ain't gonna be pretty out in them fields come mornin'."

"He wuz drunk as a skunk!" Ploox whispered.

"That's good for us," Nicky Neill stated. "It's going to be a whole lot easier to outsmart three drunks when we're ready to make our move."

"What about eet?" Pepe inquired. "Ees that job done yet?"

"Almost," Nicky Neill panted, trying to insert his tool under the stone. "There! I got it! I got it!" The rock jiggled freely in its position.

"Whut's next?" Ploox crowded closer.

"We'll pull it into the cell, but first we have to get your end up. Stick your fingers down there, Ploox. See if you can raise it."

"Okay," he huffed. "I can do it, Nicky Neill! Here goes. Ughh!" Ploox wrestled with the edge of the rock, struggling to find a niche he could work his fingers into. "There!" he cried out. "It's comin'! It's comin'!" With a coarse, grating sound, the long, heavy stone inched out of its pocket and into the cell.

"Yippee!" Nicky Neill cheered. "It's done!"

A subuded roar went up from the rest of the prisoners. But they weren't out yet.

"Sssh!" Nicky Neill cautioned them. "It's not over by a long shot. Heck, I'm not even sure I can squeeze under the door yet."

"Well, yuh better go an' finds out 'fore mornin' comes," Lawson snickered, " 'an they catches yore skinny tail stuck in that hole in the floor."

"Here goes, then." Nicky Neill dropped down on his belly and attempted to size up the opening. It was still so dark he had to rely on feel to estimate his chances. "Hmmn. Ploox, if I can get my head through I think I can make it." With great care, he tilted his head and began to guide it through the narrow space. Seconds later he stopped moving and cried out, "Ploox! Quick! Push my ear down! It's hung up!"

Ploox was right there, pressing his partner's ear under and wincing in shared pain.

"Aaaah! I'm clear ... my head's clear!"

Nicky Neill's next maneuver was to roll onto his back and begin the process of inching the rest of his body through the gap. It was tight, but not impossible. Once his shoulders were clear he brought his arms under and pushed against the bars with both hands. It was only a matter of patient squirming until his legs were free. At last, he stood up in the aisle. The dogs could no longer contain themselves. They rushed him, licking and slobbering as though he were a long lost cousin.

"I'm out! I'm really out! Campers, this is your lucky day!" Nicky Neill broke into a spontaneous jig and danced gaily in the dark with the two kid-killing hounds as eager partners. It was an unforgettable moment. Then it was back to business.

"Okay, Ploox," he stepped up to their cell door, "your turn."

CHAPTER 61

"My turn?" Ploox retreated into the cell. "Wait a minute! I ... uh ... I cain't go out there with them dogs. No way!"

"I'll hold them Ploox! I promise, they won't hurt you."

"But I might git stuck! I'm bigger 'n' you are, yuh know? You had a purty hard time gittin' under there yerself. I watched yuh."

"You can make it, Plooox. I'm sure of it."

"Well, why d'yuh need me out there anyway?"

"Because if we're going to set everyone else free we have to get the keys to the cells. It wouldn't be right if only you and me escaped. Think about Sweeney and how nuts he'd go if anybody got away."

"Yeah, okay. Yer right. So, whutta I gotta do ta git us out?"

Nicky Neill was reluctant to tell his partner the truth, but he knew there was no other way. "To free us all, you have to take the keys from Slack."

"From Slack!" Ploox's voice cracked on a high note. "Whutta yuh think he's gonna do, jus' hand 'em over ta me?" He began to pace in tight little circles beside his partner's bunk. "Look, I might crawl outta this here jail, an' even shake hands with them wolves, but there ain't no way I'll be takin' no keys from Berfel B. Slack! Whutta yuh take me for? Some kind o' hero?"

"Ploox!" Nicky Neill pressed his face between the bars. "That's exactly what I think you are ... a genuine hero. Just think about everything you've done lately and tell me if I'm wrong."

"Whut I've done?" He stopped pacing. "I ain't done nothin' but git in trouble!"

"That's what I'm talking about. For starters, you survived Slack's lightning rod more than once and never even cried."

"Hey, Ploox!" Schlink chimed in from next door. "How 'bout that Rat Dip? Anybody who can live through that's got real guts!"

"Amigo!" Now Pepe called to him. "You reesk your life wheen you jump on Slack, no? Only a reel hombre would dare such a theeng! Muchas gracias, hermano!"

"See, Ploox," Nicky Neill said, "everyone here believes in you. You're a hero! Right, guys?"

"Right!" a chorus of voices echoed in the darkness.

"And one more thing. None of this escape could have happened without you. You found the tools and smuggled them in here under the bosses' noses. That took real guts!"

"Goll-eee, did I really do all them things!"

"You bet! You're not the same old Ploox anymore. You've got a reputation now. And just think," Nicky Neill lowered his voice so only Ploox could hear, "after tonight you'll be known as the kid who led the breakout at Armadillo Ranch Camp. Somewhere down the road you might even have to sign autographs!"

"No kiddin'? All right, Nicky Neill. I'll do it. But first, tell me one thing."

"Sure. What's that?"

"Ever'one knows yer quieter 'n' me, an' braver, too. So how come you ain't goin' fer them keys?"

"It's simple. I have to hold on to these dogs, or this is as far as we get. Another thing, I want you out of that cell. If anything goes wrong at least we'll both have a chance to make a run for it. Besides, you're as brave as I am now."

"Okay, whutta I do?"

"First, you crawl out of that cell. Then you sneak up to the bosses' cabin. If Slack and Hensley are as drunk as Sweeney, they won't be hearing much of anything. Chances are, Slack will have dropped his pants off somewhere. Just find those pants and slide the keys off. And get back here! Then you can have the honor of letting everyone out. When that's done we all make a run for it. Any questions?"

"Nope. I jus' wish there wuz some other way."

"C'mon, Ploox!" The Watson brothers cheered their assurance. "You can do it!"

"We're with you all the way, man!" Jackie Simpson added his approval. A stream of encouragement followed. It was all Ploox needed.

"Okay! Okay! I'm comin' out. But if I git caught I don't want nobody mad at me. Understand?"

"Just do your best," Nicky Neill encouraged him, "and no one will blame you for anything. Come on, now! Squeeze yourself out of that coffin!"

Ploox dropped to his knees and patted the space beneath the door and the hole they had created. He sighed, rolled onto his back, and inserted his head into the crevice. Then he began to work his way under the bars. Midway through the process, as he struggled to inch his hips free, his shirt hung up behind him and jerked him to a halt. "I'm stuck!" he cried out. "Help me!"

"Push harder!" Nicky Neill urged.

"Cain't yuh gimme a hand?"

"If I do I'll have to let go of the dogs."

"Don't do that! I can do it on muh own!" With a mighty effort, Ploox forced himself ahead, stretching his T-shirt until it ripped. Seconds later he was scooching onto the aisle floor, drawing his legs after him. Free at last, he stood up and dusted himself off. "I did it!" he proclaimed. "I did it!"

Trooper and Annie growled menacingly and strained to get closer to him, but Nicky Neill held them back.

"Good job, pal. All you have to do now is keep your cool and lift those keys. I believe in you. And so do all these other guys. Our freedom is riding on you."

"Nicky Neill?" Ploox moved as close to his partner as he dared and whispered, "D'yuh really think I can do it? Hones' ta goodness?"

"Listen, I wouldn't stand out here with these dogs, waiting for you, if I didn't believe you could pull this off. Just remember two things. First, I'm sure the bosses' brains will be fogged out. Second, keep your wits about you. You stay in control up there and we'll all make history tonight. Got that?"

"Yep." He took a deep breath and everyone knew he was ready. It was now or never.

"Good luck, pal. Come on, I'll walk you to the door." With Trooper and Annie in tow, the boys shuffled over the stone slab to the exit. The barn was like a giant crypt, dark and hollow. Nicky Neill knew that once Ploox stepped outside his spirits would pick up. In the meantime, everyone else's would slip into limbo.

CHAPTER 62

When Ploox stepped out of the barn, he was stopped short by the overwhelming sense of freedom that flooded over him. A silver moon hung in the sky, embedded in a sea of sparkling stars. A moment passed. He heard an owl hooting way off in the woods and wondered if that was a good sign or not. Being alone in the dark had always scared him. Then a smile crept over his lips. No place was as black as that barn. Okay, he mused, he had to get those keys. Everyone was counting on him. He pulled his jeans up and started tiptoeing toward the bosses' cabin.

About halfway to the shack the notion struck him how much easier it was walking without that stupid chain dragging behind him. Thinking about it made him careless, though, because the next thing he knew he tripped over a root that poked above the trail. Once he regained his balance and his composure he promised himself he would pay attention to what he was doing and nothing else. A single screw-up would land them all in the Rat Dip come morning. Or worse.

Out of habit he took a swipe at his nose. For the first time ever, it was bone dry. He began to feel more confident until he spied the outline of the cabin up ahead of him. It loomed there in its own little clearing, all dark and lonesome. He couldn't help but wonder why he had ever let Nicky Neill talk him into this. It was a fool's errand, no doubt.

He crouched down behind a clump of brush and studied the place. The lights were off and he couldn't hear anyone talking. He stayed there awhile, just to be sure, listening and waiting, until his own heartbeat became so uncomfortable he couldn't stand it any longer. He tried to summon some spit, but it was no use. Despite a severe spasm of quivering in his legs, he stood up and headed for the shack.

When he reached the porch he saw there was a screen door he'd have to get past. He moved across the deck and reached for the handle. The door swung open nice and easy until about half way and then, "C - R - E - A - K!" The hinges cried out like a cat with a pinched tail. He froze right there. He just knew he'd have a heart attack if one of the meanies woke up. But nothing happened. He moved on into the room, but before he left the doorway he unhooked the spring that kept the screen shut. He couldn't bear that noise again.

By this time his eyes had adjusted to the inky shadows. The place was a disaster. Most of the furniture was spilled across the floor and there were bottles and other unrecognizable stuff laying everywhere. Walking would be a risky deal. His heart stopped cold when a hurricane snort exploded in one corner. Berfel and Cleadus were in there, okay. He knew he'd better find Berfel before Berfel found him.

He launched his search by sliding one foot across the floor and then easing the other one up beside it. He didn't want to kick anything or slip on any loose objects. He paused and attempted to focus his gaze, trying to locate Slack. With the next shift of his view he spotted a body flopped over a bench right beside him. "Hensley!" he gasped. But the dreaded foreman was dead to the world; Ploox couldn't even hear him breathing. The thunderous snort must have come from Slack. Ploox continued to move around the room until he made out a bed pushed into one corner. There was a body on it. It had to be Slack. The uncontrollable quivers intensified, only now they shook his entire body.

The shadows were so thick in the corner that all Ploox could see was an outline. But the profile of a nose told him all he needed to know. He fought the urge to hightail it and started creeping toward Slack.

"This's it," he whispered. "Git them keys an' I'm gone." After that he did his whispering in his head. One step at a time. One step at a time, he kept thinking.

The cabin was spooky beyond words and Ploox's brain began playing all kinds of tricks on him. Like, he'd see Slack's hand move, or he'd see him start to sit up, with a crazy grin on his face. Then, before he knew what had happened, his boot came down on a bottle and, "THUD!" he crashed onto the floor, butt first.

Without thinking, he bunched up into a ball and hugged the floorboards, trying his hardest to be anywhere but there. Then he heard himself breathing, gulping down air like a fish out of water. In outright panic, he sucked down a last breath and held it in. Just when he thought his chest would explode, Slack shot straight up in his bed, mumbling and grumbling to himself, "Huh? Whoozit? Whut?" Then he keeled back over and began snoring louder than a buzz saw.

Ploox begin to breathe again. But he was so scared he could have cried. He even felt his pants, but they weren't wet at all. He just knew this had to be his lucky night. Still, he lay there a while longer, wishing he was anywhere else. He wondered, too, if he would ever walk again, since his legs had turned to rubber. Pushing himself up to a crawling position, he decided to stay on all fours.

In no time, he was nose to nose with Slack. The mean-tempered jailor smelled disgusting, like dirty ashtrays and sour milk. Ploox had to move fast, before the stench made him sick. With his right hand he swept under Slack's bunk, groping for the pants he knew had to be there. No luck. He slid down to the foot of the bunk where his head collided with something solid. The whole bed quivered, but Slack kept on snoring. Ploox rose up and saw what hit him—an iron post at the end of the bunk. There was no time to worry about the lump throbbing on his forehead; he had to get back to sweeping the floor. At one point he laid down flat and swiped with both arms, but still, no pants. On the verge of absolute panic, he got up on his knees and took a closer look at Sleeping Ugly.

A skinny beam of moonlight spilled into the room from a far window, casting a thin silver line across Slack's body, cutting him in half at the waist. Ploox's eyes ran over his stubbly face, down across a hairy shoulder, past a bulging bare belly, before screeching to a halt. He'd expected to find his target passed out in his underwear, but he didn't. Instead, he came eye to eye with that blasted buckle, the one that said: THE EYES OF TEXAS ARE UPON YOU. What the heck! Slack was sleeping in his jeans!

He stared at that buckle for an eternity. Eventually, he had to face facts: if he was going to get those keys that belt had to go. Oh, Lordy, he cried to himself. What if Slack woke up? He just couldn't do it. Then his thoughts raced to all the guys down in the barn. They were counting on him. If he got caught, at least they'd know he tried. He knew then he had to do it. Slack and his buddies weren't getting any drunker lying there. In fact, one of them might have to take a pee any minute. And then he recalled what Herb had told him: "Don't be afraid of failure ... don't be afraid of failure."

Once he'd made the decision he felt a lot braver. He rose back up to his knees and reached out towards Berfel. Just to test the waters, he gave him a nudge. Nothing! He brought his other hand up and took a hold of the buckle and popped the hook out of its notch. Slack kept right on snoozing. The biggest risk was coming up. Ploox put both hands on one hip and pushed. Slack groaned, loud, and Ploox quickly ducked under the bed.

When nothing else came of it, Ploox rose up and peeked over the edge of the mattress. There was Slack, mouth open wide, flat on his back. Hallelujah! Ploox could see the keys now, spread out on the sheet by his side. He drew in a slow breath and pulled the loose end of the belt through the first two loops.

That was it. The keys slipped free, waiting to be scooped up. Ploox wrapped his fingers around the heavy ring and hoisted them clear. "So," he said to Slack, mouthing his words, "the eyes of Texas is upon me, huh? I don't mind, you ol' buzzard, 'cause yers ain't never gonna catch sight o' me again!" He stood up, walked straight out of the cabin and never looked back. All the while, the keys jingled at his side. He'd done it, by golly! He'd done it!

He kept his cool, just like Nicky Neill told him to, only now he breathed the night air like a free man. But just to stay on the safe side, he tiptoed all the way back to the jailhouse. Of course, he felt like screaming for joy when he pushed the barn door open, but he didn't. He had a reputation now.

CHAPTER 63

When the big door creaked open Jack Watson was the first to call out. "Ploox! Did ya git 'em? Did ya git 'em?"

Ploox pushed the door all the way back, allowing a shaft of moon glow to flood the entrance. Then, silhouetted in the doorway, he raised an arm into the air and jingled the key ring in response. Seconds later, he broke into an original Plucowski jig and danced down the center aisle, all the while squealing, "I got the keys, boys! I got the keys!"

"Hooray for Ploox!" Skeeter cheered, and everyone else began to shout their praise.

"Ssssh!" Nicky Neill drowned them out. "Pipe down! We're not out of here yet!" It was Ploox's finest hour and he hated to stifle it, but there was no other choice. "Great job!" he whispered to him. "No one could have done it better."

"Whut's next?" Ploox asked. He was breathless from dancing. As he spoke, he continued to jiggle the keys at his side.

"All right, we've got to work fast. Find your way to the storage room where they keep the dog food and open it up." Nicky Neill turned and addressed the cell block. "Any of you guys have stuff in that storage room?"

"No ... uh-huh," was the general response.

"We ain't got nothin' but the clothes on our backs," Nate added.

"Okay, then. Open it up, Ploox. Find our backpacks, if you can. When you're done, I'll stick the dogs in there."

It seemed to take hours for Ploox to locate the storage room key, although it couldn't have been more than a minute or two. With a crisp metallic click, the heavy door swung open.

Everyone listened while he rummaged through the dark interior, groping for the bags.

"I got 'em!" he hissed. "Bring them mutts on down."

Nicky Neill dashed for the corner, struggling to maintain control of the dogs. Trooper had already smelled food and he was beside himself to get in there.

"Okay, guys," Nicky Neill reined them in at the threshold, "the chow's all yours. Let's hope we never meet again!" He led them inside a few steps and let go of their collars. They immediately lunged for one of the feed sacks. Nicky Neill backed out right away and closed the door behind him. The last thing he heard was the two of them ripping into one of the fifty-pound bags, pawing it to shreds.

"Ploox!" he called out, spinning around. "Where are you?"

"I'm over here!" His voice echoed in the distance. "Didja lock them dogs up?"

"Yeah, no sweat. Come on, now. Let's open the cells!"

"I done got the keys ready!" he cried. "Hang on, guys! This here nightmare's almost over."

One by one, in a splendid frenzy, Ploox unlocked each cell door and swung it open wide. Each time, the grateful occupants rushed into the aisle and swarmed over him. As he moved from cell to cell the cluster of ex-prisoners at his side continued to expand, until he reached Lawson's cubicle.

"Hey! Nicky Neill!" Ploox sounded confused. "Lawson says he ain't comin'."

"He what?" Nicky Neill ran towards the cell. He had been standing by the entrance, keeping an ear out, but this news pulled him away.

"He's afraid they'll kill him if he tries to leave." It was Junior Dixon, Lawson's cellmate.

Nicky Neill couldn't believe what he was hearing. "Come on, Lawson. You can't be serious!" He pushed his way to the front of the crowd.

"I ain't goin' with y'all, an' that's that." Lawson was adamant, but his voice could not mask his fear. "Y'all's gonna git caught, sho 'nuff, an' then you boys is gonna die. Ain't no doubt in my mind."

"Come on, man!" Nicky Neill pleaded. "You're going to die here anyway, sooner or later. You've got to take this one chance. Tonight's the perfect night. Those guys are too old and too drunk to catch us once we're out."

"Lissen, they ain't so old as you think, with them dogs an' trucks o' theirs. They gonna fetch y'all outta them woods come mornin', an' then each an' every one o' you gonna be dead meat."

Nicky Neill listened to him, but all along he was recalling how much time Lawson had spent at the ranch. He was the original prisoner. He had seen other kids suffer horribly, or disappear altogether, yet he had managed to survive. Maybe that was all he was trying to do now.

"Okay, I won't try to talk you into it. I have too much respect for you. But I sure wish you would change your mind." Nicky Neill hesitated, weighing his words. "Myself, I'd rather die trying than croak in one of these cages." Without wasting any more time, he addressed Lawson's cellmate. "Jimmy Dixon, are you coming?"

"Yeah, brother. I ain't stayin' for another brekfus' in this place!"

"Well, this is it then. Everyone who's coming with me and Ploox line up by the door. Let's make our break while the getting is good."

There was a stampede for the gaping entryway where the silvery glow of the moon had pried a hole in the suffocating darkness, offering an escape shaft for those who dared to take it. As the boys crowded around the opening, peering upon a free world, Nicky Neill overheard Alvin Dodd make a final comment to Lawson.

"Jones," he called to him. "I understand yuh, but this time you're wrong. When them gorillas finds ya in here all alone they ain't gonna be pattin' ya on the back. They're gonna cave your head in for not makin' a ruckus. See, you're guaranteed some hurt if ya stay. If ya come with us, least ya got a fair chance to avoid it."

"Go on, brother," Lawson scoffed. "Y'all go yore way. I'll go mine."

Back at the door, Ploox and Nicky Neill surveyed the area a final time. All was quiet. Their moment had arrived. Nicky Neill stepped over the threshold and motioned for the others to follow. One by one, they emerged. The escape was underway.

Outside, the moon's illumination was bright enough to make Nicky Neill nervous. He stared at the dark wall in the distance. Although he couldn't distinguish much, he knew that he was looking at the first line of trees in the forest. To get there they would have to cross a wide, empty field. Once there, they would have cover and protection.

At the field's edge they bunched up in an anxious knot. "Okay," Nicky Neill said, "on the count of three we take off for the trees. Run like you've never run before, and don't look back. And no talking. Remember, we all stay together. We're going to make it! Armadillo Ranch Camp is history!"

Just then Ploox tugged at his partner's arm. "Lookit!" he gasped. "There's a light on in Sweeney's place! Whutta we do now?"

"Oh, my gosh!" Nicky Neill cried. "This is it! Come on, let's go."

Like a platoon of freedom fighters charging an enemy position, the boys burst out of the shadows and raced headlong into the open field. The precious moon glow assumed the brilliance of a prison floodlight. Each and every one of them was struck with the fear that behind that natural illuminating presence stood the machine gun images of Sweeney the Meanie and his two loathsome sidekicks. Their killer dogs would be straining at their leashes close by their sides. At any second Nicky Neill expected to feel their hot breath burning into the back of his neck.

— To Be Continued —